THIS ONE

JEAN DEGARMO

CHAPTER 1

The city of Cambridge in southeastern Ohio was sixteen miles behind Cassie as she drove toward her grandmother Eva's property. She turned right off Route 22 and up a paved hill, taking a left turn past two residences and a hobby farm before coming to Everly Road, the highest hill leading to her grandmother's 490-acre plot of land.

Up, up she drove ... until she found Grandmother's three-story Tudor-style mansion. So out of place. It was startling, even for Cassie, to see it at the top of a hill past a field of roses.

But there it was.

"The Estate," some said. Or the "grand illusion of one" others said, with its rolling front yard and cement steps buried in a row all the way up to a wood and glass front porch. Cassie's family referred to the mansion as the Tudor House or the Everly House.

And directly behind this "house" was an orchard, ten miles wide and to the right was a vegetable garden, one mile wide and equally as long. Several yards past the garden was a rectangular barn with a veranda, the interior a cache for Grandmother's collection of antiques.

I need to hurry, thought Cassie. *Or I'll die right here.*

Crash into a tree or into the guardrail at the side of the road.

She remembers two years ago in January soon after her husband Lee died; she was so lost in her memories of him, she slid off the road into a guardrail.

Thank God it's summer and the road is dry.

Thank God her Impala has air-conditioning on this brutally hot afternoon. Heat and humidity triggered her panic attacks, even more than icy roads and windstorms and almost as much as the image of her dead husband lying half broken, half rigid.

Cassie's parents said Cassie lacked the "ability to deal with conflict and change."

Like Lee dying.

Everyone thought this but Grandmother Eva.

Evalyn, pronounced Eve-ah-lyn, was Cassie's father's mother. Eva had been widowed eight years ago when her husband, Harlon, was killed in a bizarre accident. He died two days into a business trip with his friend, Harold Larrabee.

Cassie's father, Roy, said Eva used to joke about Harold and Harlon: "What a cute couple they make." Eva would tease Harlon about his "feminine" habits; his need to meet Harold once a week; never mind that he would invite Harold over to dinner, it seemed, *every time she turned around.*

Grandmother Evalyn—the family called her Eva—had only one photo of Harlon, stored away in her favorite book of poems: *The Collected Poems of Elizabeth Barrett Browning.* Cassie would take the first edition down from the bookshelf, find the faded photo of him, and study it.

He was thin and ordinary looking. Almost the same height as Eva.

Although Cassie was eighteen when he died, she wished she had paid more attention to him when he was alive, but thinking back, he wasn't around long enough for her to remember specific characteristics, and after he died, he wasn't honored in the family gallery on the walls of the red-and tan-colored sitting room.

There were hundreds of photographs, dating back to the late 1800s and early 1900s, up to the present time of 2015.

Cassie's favorite was a photo of Great-Grandfather and Great-Grandmother McClure. Great-Grandmother was sitting in a black velvet chair and Great-Grandfather was standing beside her. She was beautiful with perfectly proportioned facial features. He was confident looking, a thumb tucked into his vest. He had a handlebar moustache above his upper lip, and his expression indicated mischief.

"Such a wonderful man," Eva reminisced with tears in her eyes.

Sadly, the few memories Cassie had of *her* grandfather, Harlon, were so vague, she could only remember his peculiarities, such as his obsession with the vegetable garden: primarily, the color combination of cabbage, peas, and pumpkins.

He was obsessed with the stock market as well.

He was *brilliant* at investing Eva's money.

Cassie counted a total of 231 photos—the subjects laughing, smiling, scowling, holding hands, sitting, or standing. Dead or alive, they were displayed or shunned.

Grandfather Harlon was dead and worse than shunned. His photo was nowhere to be seen, except for page twelve of *The Collected Poems of Elizabeth Barrett Browning* "where I shoved a photo of him," said Grandmother Eva. "Shoved him away for good."

Additionally, a modest stone among the monuments of the family plot in Northwood Cemetery marked his remains. *Harlon Everett Hall: Father and Husband.*

Odd thought Cassie… He was also an uncle and grandfather. An investor. Surveyor. Geologist.

Cassie did *not* recall a funeral. She did remember a wake with food, alcohol, and laughter. Then more alcohol. Then the fond memories turned into hysterics and ultimately several people were carried out of the house.

It was such a mess.

• • •

Eva kept her wedding band in the left corner of her favorite jewelry box between two crystal figurines on top of her antique-cherry dressing table.

She gave her mother's triple-diamond engagement ring to Cassie the night before her wedding to Lee.

When Cassie was a child, Eva seemed consistently carefree and happy. She enjoyed participating in planting and pruning the gardens, determined not to let the weeds choke out her prized roses. There were so… so many roses, white, red and pink. To Cassie, Eva looked healthy and fit, not a day over forty. People thought she might be Cassie's mother, or possibly her sister. Certainly not her grandmother.

But over the past eight years since Grandfather died, Eva's chestnut-brown hair had thinned and her appetite for adventure had waned.

Cassie started shaking just thinking about Grandmother Eva, young or old.

I have to get to her.
What if she isn't home?

CHAPTER 2

Eva's father hired carpenters to build her a house after she married Harlon Hall. Her father, Ian McClure, made a fortune in coal mining from the mid-1800s to approximately 1956. He was originally from Ireland and he vowed to do whatever necessary to prosper in Guernsey County, Ohio.

Thinking of such courage, Eva would repeat the lowdown of her parents' arduous journey toward the McClure wealth by concluding: "That's how we began. And *that's* how we'll end."

Cassie rolled her eyes.

"Am I boring you, Cassandra?" she asked.

"No, Grandmother. But I've heard this before."

"And you'll hear it again. How do you think *you* got here?" With this comment, Eva would glance out the window, feeling grateful. "My father, Ian McClure, came over on a ship from Ireland to New York. He traveled from the East Coast through Pennsylvania doing odd jobs along the way to Zane's Trace, one of the first roadways through the Northwest Territory into Ohio. Midway, he met my mother, Lorraine. She was seventeen and he was eighteen. They wanted to farm, as did his family in Ireland before the great potato famine." Here Eva would shudder, close her eyes, and cross herself, although to Cassie's knowledge, she wasn't Catholic. "Father did odd jobs to survive," Eva continued. "He helped lay track for the railroad to make money for land they wanted to buy. Meanwhile, they lived in group housing—ratholes, if you will."

"I wouldn't," muttered Cassie.

"A year later, they lucked out by finding a patch of land in Guernsey County, a lush, flat-valley perfect for farming. This land was rich in coal. The coal was laying right on the surface of the ground; the very best in the area—"

Cassie interrupted: "They collected the coal on the ground and started a coal bank; they sold the coal to neighbors and the first stores in Cambridge for heat and fuel for machinery; they made a shitload of money, and when the Industrial Revolution kicked in, thanks to the railroads, Grandfather was one of the first to *deep mine* and start a coal mine company."

Eva took a deep breath.

Nonetheless, she approved of Cassie's impromptu summary. "Yes, and my father constructed the mine and eventually bought two hundred and sixty-two acres of land and built a glorious farmhouse for my mother."

"Don't forget the signature red barn," Cassie said flippantly. "The end."

"Oh, hardly the end," Eva insisted.

Over the years, the facts of their ancestral history would spring to the surface. Everyone in the family knew the story by heart.

• • •

Cassie drove onward to the back of the estate. She was anxious to see her grandmother, but knew to steel herself against possible alterations to her life.

There was always an addendum Eva wanted to discuss with her: a change in the landscaping (usually floral), a renovation to her house, or a "tweak" to her last will and testament.

Just like Grandfather Harlon's obsession with the stock market and his job, thought Cassie, there is something equally mysterious about Eva's preoccupation with her will and her roses.

Eva was seventy-four years old, or at least that's what Cassie had been told. She exercised daily, mostly by walking the grounds, inspecting her rose gardens and overseeing the progress of Harlon's massive orchard. Her personal maintenance man, Eric (Cassie could never remember his last name, although she had known him since they were children), owned and worked for an appliance repair company seven miles away in Byesville.

Eva had depended on Eric for the past year and a half. He would come at the drop of a hat if summoned by her, usually regarding problems related to plumbing, electrical, and adjusting or replacing gadgets on appliances. Like his father, Steven, before him, Eric would come immediately for Eva, even if on the clock with his regular job.

Eva paid him well, but for the most part Eric stayed loyal to her because his father had been her right-hand man. When his father retired, Eric took over.

"Always remember, if you need someone to come for *any* reason, especially in an emergency, call Eric." Again, Cassie couldn't recall his last name. Something beginning with Saint—Saint John, Saint Clair, Saint *something*.

"Like his father," Eva continued, scrunching her forehead and narrowing her blue eyes, "he's the keeper of our keys, and believe me, he has one to every entrance."

Cassie couldn't help but stare at Eva. Maybe it was the idea of Eric having a key to *every* entrance. Maybe it was Eva's determination to forbid any maintenance person other than Eric on the estate.

• • •

As Cassie's father, Roy, said more than once, "My parents were made for each other, down to the similarity of their height, weight, and pale blue eyes."

But Grandmother Eva had the money. She inherited the coal mines from her parents and invested the profits well. Her parents had owned the 262 acres of land near their one mine on Cleary Road in Center City Township and built a homestead—a farmhouse, a red barn, and two sheds—which Eva sold after her father passed away.

After Ian McClure died from a heart attack, Eva's mother, Lorraine, lived with Eva and Harlon in the Tudor House until Lorraine died four years later of a stroke.

Sitting in her car, Cassie surveyed the lawn, so lush and green. She studied the serpent-like shapes of the bushes lining the sidewalk up to the porch.

The trees, now vibrant with green leaves, stood in perfect lines in the backyard and along the sides of the house. The plant life would take turns blooming, but this time of year, most of the flowers were fully bloomed. The purple rhododendron; blue, yellow, and orange daylilies— Eva's favorite other than her roses—the red and pink columbine; white and blue lupines . . . there was a magnificent blending of colors and shapes.

Cassie took a deep breath and told herself, "You can make it to the porch and into the kitchen."

Then she started to cry, hysterically, with difficulty breathing, although the air conditioner was on high.

She pulled her handbag from the passenger seat and rummaged for her cell phone. It would be crazy to phone Grandmother, but she would if she had to.

There was a tap on the window. She turned and focused on Eric What's-His-Name.

He made a fist and thumped the window again. "Cassie," he yelled. "Look at me!"

Looking into his hazel eyes forced her to concentrate on what he was saying. There was a bandana tied around his forehead over his curly brown hair. He was tall and slim and had prominent facial features, especially his cheekbones and nose. His complexion was light-brown from working outside, a shade darker on his hands and arms.

"Open the door," he yelled.

Cassie's hair, a light-brown, almost blonde, was held back with a hair tie. She straightened the front of her sleeveless white blouse and pulled at her ponytail. "No," she said through the window. "I can't!"

She sensed Eric did not understand the concept of "I can't" which also told her he would never be able to comprehend an anxiety attack of this dimension. He was a hard worker. No slacker. His face told this story by the scar on his chin and the creases near his eyes.

Eva claimed Eric was like his father. *He was raised to work in severe weather conditions: heat, blizzards, humidity, ice, and rain.*

10

"Unlock the door," Eric said, "and I'll help you!"

Cassie pushed the lock button. Eric opened the door and reached past her to turn the key in the ignition. Sudden silence. She cried harder, so he took her arm and helped her out to the driveway and into the heat.

She stumbled across the brick patio, to the back steps and into the never-ending, so-white-it-hurt-her-eyes interior of the back porch. Three ceiling fans spun over her head, generating an immediate cooldown. She found a Kleenex in her pocket and wiped her eyes.

She could feel the blessed breeze of the ceiling fans lined up in a row, replacing the hot, stale air. She saw pots of green ferns quivering on tables near white wicker rocking chairs and blue high-back chairs.

Cassie almost tripped as she ran through the porch into the kitchen. *The kitchen is too big,* she thought. *I'll never make it. Everything here is too big and too white.*

Cassie tried to call out for Grandmother or even Grandmother's assistant, Frances Winthrop, but her throat was so dry she couldn't swallow, much less speak.

Watch out for the tile floor in the kitchen.

"Cassie," said Frances. "What's wrong with you?"

"Frances, is that you?" The tears in Cassie's eyes warped her vision. "Frances?"

Frances studied Cassie from the louvered double-door closet where she had just deposited a mop and a bucket.

"Are you being chased?" Frances asked, her scowl suggesting the question had been painful for her to think, let alone say.

Cassie leaned against the industrial-sized oven to catch her breath. She could hear her father wail: "That damn oven!

Why does Mother need to keep it when no one lives in that absurd mausoleum but her!"

Cassie's father, Roy, had taken to calling the Tudor-style mansion a 'mausoleum' soon after his father passed away.

"Well, she loves it, it's her home!" Rachel, Cassie's mother, would say.

But Cassie knew what her mother was really thinking: *Sell the house and all the land! Big profit... Big profit!*

"My father wouldn't approve of that enormous oven or buying fancy furniture and wasting money on gardens and foo-fah flowers!" Roy would roar.

Grandfather wouldn't care, thought Cassie.

Because one thing Cassie *did* remember: Grandfather followed Eva's orders.

Cassie turned her attention back to Frances, who stood smug in lime-green capris and a short-sleeved purple blouse, wearing a handkerchief to keep her ratty gray hair out of her eyes. Her ugly feet were stuffed into white, scuffed-up sandals. "Lunchtime's over," she said.

Cassie felt sick just by looking at her, mostly due to the chipped, bright-red polish plastered across Frances's toenails.

Cassie fought the urge to back away when she realized Frances held out a glass of water for her to take. "Thank you," she said.

"Your grandmother's upstairs in her bedroom," Frances murmured. She waited for Cassie to drink the water and hand the glass back before disappearing into the sitting room off the kitchen.

At the same time, Eric reappeared, as if emerging from the ivory-colored appliances. "There you are," he said. "Why did you take off?"

"Oh, I—" She stopped talking and started thinking, *why would he care? It's strange for him to even—*

"Never mind," he said. "At least you're okay. I fixed the back gate for your gramma. Tell her for me when you see her. I have to get back to the shop."

He always called Eva "Gramma."

When Eric disappeared again, Cassie checked the inside of the refrigerator for something to eat, thinking food might stop her shaking. She found a plastic bottle of grape juice and miniature egg and ham salad sandwiches leftover from Grandmother's porch party two nights ago.

If Grandmother is upstairs in her bedroom, why do I hear footsteps above to the right, possibly in one of the guestrooms, past the library and the two bathrooms?

She ate the last of the tiny sandwiches and moved towards the hallway. She stopped when out of nowhere came Frances's shadow. Frances's jagged silhouette grew taller and moved over to the alcove leading to a hallway under the staircase.

The sunlight reflected off the copper ceiling medallions, which meant the draperies in the living room were wide open. Mahogany pocket-doors lined the walls—two for storage and four more leading to other areas of the house.

Cassie peered into the main library beneath the stairway. No one there. She touched the beige wallpaper . . . traced the oval designs with a finger. She wasn't sure what the designs symbolized and didn't care. Too fancy anyway.

Then, with one hand pressed against the wall, she paused to listen . . . nothing.

Where did Frances go? The sliding footsteps had to be Frances's. A clip-clop, slip-shuffle of cheap sandals against the hardwood floor.

Cassie heard a door slam. Next a screen door slapped shut, and again, she heard two sets of footsteps, one on both ends of the upstairs hallway.

Finally, she made it to the top of the stairway. She held her breath to listen. The central air hummed; otherwise, the house was quiet except for a plop, plop and a lighter tap on the other side of the upstairs level.

Then there was a crash, like glassware had been tossed or pitched. And a shriek. But not Grandmother's. No. Grandmother would never shriek like a damsel in distress.

Grandmother would go for the double-barrel shotgun next to her bed.

CHAPTER 3

Cassie sat down on the third step from the top of the stairway. She couldn't move. Couldn't breathe. *Grandmother is dead. I know it.*

Such horrific silence, like never before. Then a rattling noise from upstairs. On the second floor, or the third? There was a light oscillating from the bay window in the living room all the way around to a direction far beyond her. Back and forth. "Grandmother!" she whispered, but meant to shout.

Cassie felt like she had been sedated; and she was terrified of drugs. After Lee died, she refused to take a mild anti-anxiety medication suggested by the family doctor. She vowed to work through her grief, not around it.

But over the last four months, her depression had taken on a life of its own with a gradual paralysis of her body and mind. Like now. She could *not* stand up, or even slide to the floor beneath her. She was frozen on the third step from the top of the stairway.

In the shadows she could see Lee lying dead in the coroner's office, the very breath and light knocked out of him. His forehead crushed.

Lee was traveling on 270 toward Columbus. He was to assess a lucrative property for insurance purposes for a colleague who asked him to double-check the land his uncle's company wanted to buy. *Office buildings,* she thought bitterly. The autopsy report concluded he had a heart attack due to a heart defect.

He was only twenty-eight.

More noises, like furniture moving and scraping but Cassie couldn't imagine Grandmother ruining the hardwood floor or the carpet by pushing furniture across it.

Cassie stood and forced herself up the last two steps. She grabbed the banister for leverage. *Why is it so hot in here?* she wondered. *Did that stupid Frances turn the air-conditioning off?*

She made it to the top. She should have eaten more, but she didn't have much of an appetite since Lee died. They were so young when they married—Cassie twenty-two and Lee twenty-four. They had only been married for four years.

But now she was motivated by the fear that her grandmother was hurt. Grandmother spent a lot of time in her bedroom, but not the same one she had shared with Grandfather Harlon. After he died, she moved farther down the hallway to the second from the last bedroom on the right. There was a room attached to Eva and Harlon's former bedroom for Grandmother McClure, who was living with them before she got sick. They renovated both rooms to include a sitting room for Grandmother McClure, but now the sitting room was Eva's library.

Cassie walked down the hallway and pushed open the door that had been left ajar. And there she was—Grandmother Eva—sitting at her dressing table, putting on makeup, focusing on her nose.

Through the reflection in the three-way mirror, Eva realized Cassie was watching her. "Cassandra!" she shouted; her voice uncommonly deep. "What on earth!"

"I heard noises. I was downstairs in the kitchen and heard thumping and crashing sounds."

"As far as I know, I'm the only one here," said Eva, her back still to Cassie.

Eva was tucking her brownish-gray hair under a cap. She wore dark pants and a lavender-colored blouse with the sleeves rolled up to the elbow.

"I have gardening to do," she said. "Maybe Frances hasn't left yet. She made lunch and said she had errands to run. Cassandra!" Eva stood up and pushed the ottoman of her dressing table to the side. "What's wrong with you?"

Grandmother was quick to her feet, always had been, as far back as Cassie could remember. When Lee died, it was Grandmother who helped Cassie sort through his items and arrange the funeral and luncheon afterwards. It was Grandmother who cleaned up Lee's debt.

Eva helped Cassie over to her canopy bed. The bed was so high, Eva had to help Cassie up onto the mattress, which wasn't too difficult. Cassie only weighed 115 pounds— thin for her stature.

"You have to get a hold of yourself, Cassandra," Eva chastised. "I'm getting sick of saying it! If you keep up like this, you'll die!"

Cassie rolled onto her side and faced the bathroom door instead of Grandmother. She had heard this speech before. She was tired of life in general and Grandmother just didn't get it.

Nonetheless, something struck Cassie as peculiar. "You never garden this late in the day. You always said it's too hot this time of day to work outside!"

Eva rubbed Cassie's shoulder until Cassie turned to look at her. "Cassandra, I'm going out to inspect the grounds. You must get a hold of yourself. You're young. You have your whole life ahead of you. Lee wouldn't want you to grieve all these years after his death. He would want you to take care of business. For both of you."

"It's only been two years!" Cassie cried. "I can't go on without him!"

"But you *have* been! You still go to your job at the insurance company every day. You need to start eating better. You—"

"I quit my job yesterday," Cassie yelled to the wall. "I can't concentrate anymore."

"I see. Then maybe you should move in here with me for a week or so. Until you get motivated again."

"No! I'll never leave our home. Lee and I picked it out together."

Eva sat down on the edge of the bed. "You should sell it and find a smaller house. I'll hire you as my manager."

Eva pulled a handkerchief from her blouse pocket and shoved it into Cassie's hand.

"Manage *what* exactly?" Cassie sounded sarcastic and knew it. "Manage the gardens? Manage the fleet of expensive vehicles in the two garages? Manage the ghosts?"

"What ghosts, Cassandra?"

"The voices I hear every time I come here, Grand-mother. You have to be deaf not to hear voices and all the noise! Glass breaking and dishes smashing against walls! Furniture dragged across the floor!"

She realized Eva was staring at her. *She thinks I'm crazy,* Cassie thought. *I've gone too far.*

Eva stood from the side of the bed and turned to get her cell phone on the dressing table. "I'm calling Doctor Benley. This has gone on long enough. You need help."

Cassie grabbed Eva's wrist. "I won't take drugs!"

"No one said anything about drugs!" Eva shouted. "You need help. You're hallucinating and hearing things. No one has been here all day except for Frances and myself. I had lunch with Frances before she left on errands."

"Eric was here," said Cassie. She sat up on the bed. "I saw him outside when I got here. He said to tell you he fixed the back gate."

Eva put a hand to her forehead, apparently revisiting her recent phone conversations. "I haven't talked to Eric for at least a week. I don't like not knowing who's prowling around without my consent."

Cassie knew Eva wouldn't put the call into Dr. Benley now that her mind was on Eric.

Cassie was up and out of the bed. "I thought you trusted Eric. What's been happening, Grandmother? *Tell me.*"

"No one has been breaking into the house, as far as I know. But there have been things missing. Equipment, bags of mulch. And the side door of the garage was unlocked the day before yesterday. Just minor issues."

Grandmother had always been a practical woman, not a paranoid one.

But Cassie noticed something crucial was missing in the corner near the closet. "Where's your shotgun, Grandmother?"

Eva's hand fell from her throat into a fist. "Good question," she said. "It was there last night."

CHAPTER 4

Cassie was determined to find Eric and ask him why he had lied to her. Why did he say Grandmother asked him to fix the back gate? Grandmother wasn't senile or incapacitated. If anything, she would pull the cord on her own life when she was good and ready.

Cassie told Eva she would drive back to Eighth Avenue in Cambridge, get some of her necessities, and return to the house as soon as possible.

Every time she parked in the driveway at her home on Eighth, she choked back the memory of Lee looking out the window, waiting for her. He was always home first when their work day ended. He would stand in the window and wave to her as she parked her car behind his truck.

Now she hated the house. She hated the yard he mowed in the summer and raked in the fall. She hated the bright cheery kitchen with yellow wallpaper.

Suddenly, she felt relieved about quitting her job, and thankfully, she had eight thousand dollars in her savings. She would use this money sparingly to pay her bills. When she felt up to it, she would put this drafty old house needing a coating of paint on the market.

Be done with it. And done with Lee.

She unlocked the kitchen door by the driveway. As always, it was cold inside, even in the winter with the electric heat on high. *Cold, because I'm as dead as my husband.*

She dropped her handbag onto the square table and walked down the hallway to the master bedroom, where she quickly pulled T-shirts, shorts, and underwear out of her dresser. Silly of her, but Lee's things were just as he had left them, folded neatly in his section of the dresser.

She packed slippers and nightshirts, tennis shoes, makeup, some jewelry. She didn't need her pricey work outfits anymore; that part of her wardrobe is history.

She had enjoyed her job as an insurance claims adjuster and clerk typist, but now she won't have to worry if a panic attack seized her in public.

Before leaving the bedroom, she went to the dresser, opened the top drawer, and took out Lee's watch and his wedding ring. She wore her wedding ring all the time, along with her diamond engagement ring.

She didn't need or want anything else in the house. She would decide what furniture to keep and what to discard when she was ready to put the house on the market.

In the kitchen, she found a paper bag and packed coffee, cereal, bottled water, and laundry detergent, as an afterthought. More like a necessity in case Grandmother's pantry wasn't well stocked. Cassie would do the grocery shopping while staying with Grandmother. That ugly witch Frances would have to take a back seat.

• • •

"Frances told me your gramma wanted the back gate fixed," said Eric when Cassie confronted him at the St. James Repair Shop on the outskirts of Byesville. "It looked okay to me, but I replaced the top right hinge and tightened the handle."

Cassie leaned against the service counter. She looked around the store, thinking how lucky he was that his father, who had been retired for months, signed the business over to Eric.

Cassie knew from Eva that Eric's father, Steven, had built up and improved the appliance shop through the years with help from the McClures and other businesspeople in the area. Thus, St. James Repair Shop was a prosperous, vital addition to Byesville and surrounding cities like Cambridge, Coshocton, and Zanesville.

Cassie thought, *it was a community effort.*

"What's so funny?" Eric asked.

"Nothing. I was just thinking how your shop has grown over the years."

"My dad and Uncle Jim worked hard to make it happen. I helped them when I was old enough." He was preoccupied inventorying nuts and bolts in the cubbyhole display behind the counter.

Cassie noticed he had changed clothes since her melt-down earlier at Grandmother's. He now wore a blue short-sleeved shirt and olive-green work pants. His hair was neatly combed, but in her opinion, too wavy and long around his ears and neck. He was six foot two, she guessed, although he was wearing some type of boot.

"You were a bully in high school," she pointed out.

"And you were a bitch," he said.

Eric doesn't have the proper personality to work in customer service, thought Cassie. She wondered how he interacted with his customers on-site, in their homes or businesses, fixing washing machines, dryers, refrigerators.

"The thing is, my grandmother said she didn't *ask* you to fix the gate," Cassie said. "She also said someone's been breaking into the garage and sheds. Stealing things. Do you know anything about that?"

Eric dropped the notebook onto the marbled surface of the countertop. "Are you accusing me of something?"

His cell phone rang and he answered it. "St. James Repair," he said in a congenial voice.

Cassie made her way to the front of the store. When she opened the glass door, a bell rang above her head, and the next thing she knew, she was out into the heat again, even though it was evening and the heat had eased down a notch. Still, she thought she was going to faint.

As she walked along the pavement, hoping not to see insects or sticky substances on the sidewalk, she decided that yes, Eric had lied to her.

• • •

Back at the house again, after parking her car in the main garage, Cassie made her way up the steps to the back-porch door. She carried one suitcase. The suitcase was heavier than she had anticipated, and she wanted to leave it on

the brick patio but decided someone might steal it. Most of her necessities—makeup, hair dryer, medication, 300 dollars in cash, and her checkbook—were inside this suitcase.

She dragged the heavy suitcase up the steps and onto the back porch. As far as she knew, she was alone.

But one can never be sure.

She turned the main light on in the kitchen. She heard the hum of the double-door refrigerator. There was the strong scent of disinfectant, telling her that Frances had been on the premises within the past hour.

Frances must know who's making all the racket upstairs on the opposite side of Grandmother's bedroom. For years, Grandmother wanted Frances to live with her, but Frances insisted on living in her own house near the park in Cambridge. Frances had never married and preferred her privacy.

That way she can come and go after making trouble for Grandmother and her family, thought Cassie.

Once again, Cassie climbed the steep stairway without taking a break. Grandmother always had night-lights on throughout the upstairs and downstairs of the house. Cassie found the way, thanks to these tiny lights.

She made it to the right of the stairway, one bedroom away from Grandmother's. She would have *her* privacy, yes, but she would also be able to hear if something terrible happened to Grandmother.

Or so she believed.

CHAPTER 5

Harlon Hall met Eva in May of 1958. The Korean War ended in 1953. He been a part of the war, but state side. He was trained as a geologist and also in clerical and soon after the war ended, he completed a degree in geology.

Harlon was exceptional at his profession. He thrived on examining various faults—granite, quartz, formations of mountains, hills—via the glaciers of long ago in degrees of depth and width, throughout every part of the world.

In 1837, the Ohio Legislative established the Geological Survey. The Geological Survey inspected and documented mineral resources in specific areas. Harlon was involved in the mapping and the distribution of these minerals. He was also involved in locating abandoned underground coal mines. He was sought after by independent coal mine owners. One in particular was Ian McClure, and through McClure, Harlon met Evalyn.

Harlon respected McClure well enough to be cautious when it came to his daughter. He knew very well how the mine owners regarded the unions, particularly the United Mine Workers Association. Harlon knew that early on, men like McClure hired Pinkerton guards to block or settle disputes between the substitute (scab) workers hired out of the county and the local striking laborers. He knew that men like McClure were difficult to crack, but over the short time he had worked for McClure Mining, he could see a change was forthcoming. Even Ian McClure would gradually agree to higher wages and safer working conditions. Times were changing in the mining industry, and intelligent, successful businessmen like McClure knew how and when to adapt.

Harlon was part of the team hired by McClure and two other mine owners in the Tri-State area to survey and locate viable coal prospects.

Eventually, Eva's appearance in the office caught Harlon's attention. She wore trousers and matching work shirts. She wore steel-toed boots, and caps upon her chestnut-brown hair, which was medium-length and wavy below her ears. Her eyes, he noticed, were pale blue like his own. Her eyes, however, were more of an almond shape and his were round.

You exciting, mysterious woman! he thought. And attractive, in a mannish way, although she had full lips, a small nose, and from what he could tell beneath her outfit, a curvy figure.

She was always with her father when he inspected the mines. She scribbled notes on a clipboard as they toured the mining town where the workers and their families lived.

Harlon soon noticed that twice a week Eva helped out in the grocery store. She would take the scrips allotted to each family from the wives and fill their orders. It didn't appear to matter to her that the workers were poorly treated with low wages and pitiful living conditions. Or that the women and children wore clothes resembling rags.

She is a business woman, foremost, thought Harlon. *She's dedicated to helping her father build his wealth and those. on the other side of the fence are not her worry.*

"Hello," he said to the back of her head. "I'm Harlon Hall. Hired by your father to survey mining prospects." She was arranging canned goods on a shelf. "I'm a geologist," he added, thinking she might be deaf. Or faking that she was. "I'm from Cleveland, and I'm an orphan, unfortunately." He hoped the orphan comment might get her attention. He never knew his parents— a confirmed fact.

But she focused on the clipboard atop the counter and jotted down numbers. Finally, she turned to look at him, and he wondered if she noticed the similarity of their blue eyes.

"Is that right?" she said. "Good to meet you." She extended her hand to him. Her skin felt similar to a man's—not exactly rough, but close.

"You're Evalyn McClure. I admire your father a great deal," he added. "I noticed you spend a lot of time here, helping with the business. Are you an heir to this establishment?"

He felt the muscles in his mouth expand to a grin.

He saw her lose interest in him with two blinks and a frown. "And," she said before walking to the back of the store, "I won't forget you asked."

She never did.

She never, *ever* let him forget how she knew from the beginning he was after her father's money.

Plan B: Harlon decided to woo Eva *through* her. father, Mr. McClure, which is what Harlon called him even after the old man's death.

Harlon respected McClure's story—how he traveled from Ireland to New York to Pennsylvania to Zane Trace, all the way to the bottom of the Appalachian Trail to Guernsey County where, by luck, by chance, by circumstance, he stopped at an area and claimed it as his own. Maybe God led Ian McClure to the patch of land in Guernsey County, rich in coal on the surface, to be gathered and, yes, dig deeper. Always, always dig deeper.

CHAPTER 6

Cassie chose the bedroom down the hallway from Grandmother's. The bedroom she wanted, next to Grandmother's, was occupied with clothing, boxes of dishes, unused furniture, and other cast-off items. Cassie imagined a huge garage sale, but a garage sale was the last thing Grandmother would allow.

Maybe, thought Cassie, they could donate items, or sell some of the jewelry, paintings, and furniture on eBay.

Hardly. Grandmother would throw a fit.

Cassie relaxed after rearranging the furniture in her room: a rocking chair, a bed, and a dresser. She would keep this room, temporarily. She had forgotten how fun it was as a child to explore all the rooms in Grandmother's house.

Cassie suspected there were hidden doorways to hidden stairways, but she never pursued the concept of hidden *rooms*. She would soon enough. A hidden room would be perfect for her important papers and her favorite pieces of jewelry.

She made the queen-sized bed with sheets and a comforter she had found in the walk-in closet. She liked the colors: pink and white. A cheerful atmosphere, as opposed to the dreary blue and brown of the bedroom she used to share with Lee.

She had to push thoughts of Lee away if living with Grandmother for a few days and starting over was going to work.

The carpet beneath her feet was sea-green and soft. She liked how it coordinated with the pink and white colors. She kicked off her flats, feeling even more comfortable about settling in, especially when the purr of the air-conditioning started up again.

She unpacked some of the clothes she brought from her house on Eighth Avenue but panicked while thinking about the rest of the items she still had to bring to Grandmother's. She would include most of the furniture and appliances with the house when she put it on the market.

Grandmother knew all of the top real estate agents in the area. She told Cassie once that through Grandfather Harlon's best friend, Harold Larrabee, who had been a successful land developer and partnered with Grandfather in buying properties in the Cleveland and Columbus area, there was never a need to go further than Grandmother's address book when shopping for property or a home.

Cassie finished unpacking, changed into a T-shirt and pajama shorts, and climbed into bed.

• • •

The next morning, after Cassie got up, put on a robe, and made her way down the stairs, she overheard part of a conversation before walking into the kitchen. She heard Frances say, "You can't let her live here! What's wrong with you?"

"She's my granddaughter, you ingrate!" said Grandmother in a searing voice. "We can manage for a week or two. You can just—" She stopped talking when she saw Cassie standing in the doorway. "Hello, Cassandra. Come in and have coffee with us."

Cassie went over to the coffee maker and selected a cup. Grandmother hated heavy mugs, so one would find china cups on the shelves and in the cupboards, some lighter and daintier than others.

Cassie poured coffee into a lavender cup with blue trim. She mixed in creamer from a glass pitcher on the counter and stirred in two spoons of sugar.

She turned to Frances. "Maybe *you* should be the one to leave."

Frances lips slid toward a chin with two moles and a patch of whiskers.

Cassie looked away.

The woman truly made her sick to her stomach. Just the unkempt, dowdy appearance of her . . . the crust at the sides of her mouth.

"Oh my," said Grandmother.

"Never!" said Frances.

Cassie nudged Frances's arm with her own as she walked past the island counter in the center of the kitchen. She chose a chair, and Grandmother sat down in the chair across from her.

Grandmother was dressed in cotton denim pants and a yellow blouse with the sleeves rolled up to the elbows. There was a purple striped visor slanted upon her head.

Grandmother cleared her throat. "Frances is worried you will become a recluse," she said. "She's *very* worried about you."

Cassie looked over at Frances, who stood like a humped-back skeleton in oversized clothes. Her hair was wispy above her tiny orange ears.

"Really, Fran?" Cassie chided. "That's so nice of you. I'll take pancakes and bacon. Orange juice too. And if you wouldn't mind, please make it fresh squeezed."

Grandmother snorted and crossed her arms. "I'll have the same, Frances."

Cassie detected a ripple of resentment move across Frances's face, but Frances turned and walked to the counter, taking her scowl and her smacking lips with her.

• • •

After breakfast, Grandmother left the house to inspect her rose gardens. Cassie went back upstairs to sort through her financial papers, thinking she should cash in some stocks and deposit more money into her savings account. She would check her balances and then call her father, who was educated in investing. But first, she would have to tell him she had quit her job, and that piece of news would make him furious.

Her father, Roy, was fifty-six years old. He had a bachelor's degree in electrical engineering and another bachelor's in accounting. He traveled a lot for his job. He didn't seem to mind being away from home two out of four weeks per month. Cassie's mother, Rachel, didn't mind either. Rachel had picked up memberships to prestigious charity groups and she was a board member of both the hospital and the local library in Cambridge, positions of high esteem that Eva passed on to her after Harlon died.

Rachel was trained as a licensed practical nurse, but quit her job when she married Roy. She knew an income from *her* wasn't warranted to support their lavish lifestyle or her peace of mind.

She gave birth to Cassie and wanted another baby but suffered two miscarriages. After a year of trying, she decided to close shop. Her heart couldn't take the trauma of another miscarriage, and she was getting too old (pushing fifty) to have another baby anyway.

When Cassie called her parents' house, she was thankful Rachel didn't answer the phone.

Her father answered, and Cassie came straight to the point. "I need to speak with you about my stock. I want to cash some in."

"I wouldn't advise that," Roy said between gasps of air. Cassie pictured him puffing away on a long cigarette. "You need to let it ride. All your stocks are safe moneymakers."

"How would you know?"

Roy chuckled, puffed a bit more. "Because I check them regularly. That's how I know!"

When Lee died in the car wreck, it was Father who went with Cassie to view his body at the morgue. Granted, Eva helped Cassie with all the arrangements and paid for everything, including the ornate casket, but at the time, Roy was a steadfast force for Cassie.

Roy held Cassie upright when she said goodbye to Lee's body. The shell of Lee ... disfigured from the accident.

Nonetheless, Roy insisted that she *not* sell any stocks.

She had no choice but to put it bluntly: "I need ready cash, Father. To move into my savings. I quit my job at the insurance agency."

There was a wheeze and a cough, an ear-splitting choke.

"Why the *hell* did you do that, Cassandra?" he demanded to know.

"I couldn't take it any longer! I moved in with Grandmother for a few days."

"You moved in with *Eva*?" Roy asked. "With *Eva*?" he asked again, as if his own mother was a contagious disease, sure to kill them all.

"I don't think that's a good idea, Cassandra!" he shouted after catching his breath. "You need an income; you need to keep busy! And you *have* a house of your own!"

"I'm going to put it on the market," Cassie shouted back. "I can't live there anymore! I just can't!" At this point, she started to cry, the repetitive, panting noise she couldn't help but make whenever she lost control. A surge of anxiety overwhelming her when she least expected.

"Honey!" Roy blurted into his cell phone. "Come over today and we'll discuss a reasonable plan."

"I'm bringing Grandmother," Cassie said, decisively. "I want Grandmother with me!"

"So be it," Roy said before hissing. And he hung up.

CHAPTER 7

E va refused to go with Cassie. She claimed that she was too busy, and the last thing she wanted to do was to go to her son's house. "Besides," she said, garden basket in hand, "they are invited here for dinner Sunday afternoon. Please remind them, Cassandra."

The brief encounter with Grandmother had taken place in the driveway before Cassie drove off to her parents' house near New Concord. Father, having been an alumnus of Muskingum University, insisted on living near his alma mater. But the main distinction about New Concord was that it was John Glenn's birthplace.

Father was proud of this fact.

Cassie cranked the air conditioner. It was going to be a scorching- hot August overall, according to the weather man on the local radio station. *Only August fifth,* he said, *but the real heat is yet to come.*

The *real* heat? Cassie felt sick to her stomach already, despite the cool air blasting from the vents by her feet and arms. She gripped the steering wheel, thinking of the errands she had to run after meeting with her father, and lucky for her, he normally ate lunch at home. Luckier still, Cassie noticed, her mother's silver Corvette wasn't parked at the right side of the four-car garage in its usual spot.

Cassie ran into the sprawling ranch-style house. "Father!"

"In here, Cassie!" he shouted from somewhere down the hallway.

Cassie went to his study where she found him on his hands and knees. "*What's* going on?" she asked his bent back, but when she got closer, she realized he was dealing with a dark stain on the light-brown carpeting.

According to his body language, the pumping of his elbows in particular, he was frantic. "What have you done?" she asked, now close enough to identify blood.

"I was hanging a picture on the wall and it fell. The glass broke and cut me. Right in the goddamned leg!" He finished cleaning and stood up, favoring his left leg.

He shrugged the mishap off, as if to say, *It's just one of those things!*

"You've lost a lot of blood," said Cassie. "That's not good!"

He was wearing gray shorts, and strings of blood had mixed in with the black hairs on his leg. "Oh shit, honey!" he said. "Really! It's nothing!"

Her father wasn't one to say things like "oh shit."

Now Cassie was really concerned.

Especially when she saw the half-empty bottle of bourbon on his desk.

"I have your paperwork here," he said, indicating the portfolio on his desk by a stack of receipts and invoices. "I've gone over it all again, Cassandra, and I don't think it's wise for you to sell."

He hobbled to his desk and fell into the padded chair. "Not right now, anyway," he added, slipping black-framed glasses onto his nose.

"I *need* to," she said. "I quit my job."

"So you said," he spat. "So -you-said!"

Cassie watched him press a paper towel against the wound. "Father, I think you should go to the ER and get your leg checked. Please. It might get infected."

"Nothing major," he interrupted. "Nothing major," he repeated. "Just a cut that will heal in time."

Cassie knew that if her father said going to the ER wasn't in the cards, no one could change his mind. Besides, she also knew he was more worried about Rachel finding the stain on the carpeting. It didn't matter that the stain happened in Father's private office. A stain is a stain.

Cassie changed the subject. She knew what he was going to ask next and she intended to beat him to it. "I'm not taking money from Grandmother, if that's what's on your mind!"

Why? she was thinking, *is father's chest hair gray, sticking out of his white, short-sleeved shirt? Why has he gained so much weight?*

He used to care about his appearance, but lately, it's as if the buttons down the front of his shirt are about to pop. He used to go to the fitness club and work out twice a week; now his skin is flabby and he has an extended stomach.

Cassie didn't approve of his shaggy appearance or his slurred words. She flexed her thoughts back to her mother's indiscretions. "Where's Mother?"

"Visiting friends in Zanesville," he said. "Now you look here! Let the stocks go, honey. Give it another two months and if you still feel the same way, we'll select a few low riders to cash in."

He'd call stocks that were losing instead of gaining low riders. Cassie used to think it was funny. Not anymore.

She wanted to protest, but he pushed a check across the cluttered desk. "You earned this a year ago when you helped your mother at the library sale. And you earned it when you participated in the glass museum fundraiser. Mother agrees with me to give you this check!"

When he was on point with a thought, he would not or could not control his voice. "He's theatrical," said Grandmother Eva. "He thinks he's on stage. Like his father."

"Listen to me!" Cassie started to protest, but after reflecting back to the three boring days she spent helping with the museum fundraiser, yes, she would take the check.

"I just can't—"

"Oh, you will!" Roy yelled, sweating profusely despite the cool air whirling through the vents. "Yes, you will!"

She picked up the check but decided not to look at it until she was in her car. She wasn't in the mood to meet up with her mother, knowing that "meeting her friends in Zanesville" translated to Mother coming home tipsy.

Cassie said from the door, "I wish you would get that wound checked out!"

Roy lifted the wad of paper towel to show her. "The bleeding has stopped! Marvelous!" When he looked at her and winked, there were veins sticking out of his forehead and she noticed his cheeks were beet-red. "Marvelous!" he repeated, showing his big white teeth.

He was terribly vain about his teeth.

He was also vain about his hair, which was piled into a wavy pompadour above his ears.

Cassie backed into the hallway. "Goodbye, Father. Don't forget to come to Grandmother's house Sunday afternoon for dinner!"

"Oh, sure, sure, "he mumbled.

But she knew he hadn't heard her.

"Sunday afternoon!" she yelled into the chilly room before closing the door.

• • •

The check was for five thousand dollars. She went to her bank and deposited all but four hundred dollars into her checking account. Now she could pay her cell phone bill and buy a few essentials.

She went to her house to collect the mail that was bulging from the mailbox. She must go to the post office and get her mail transferred to Grandmother Eva's box number.

Cassie's mind was made up about selling her house. She needed the money. She knew it was time to move and she would stay at Grandmother's until she found a new house, *if* she decided to stay in the Cambridge area. She might move to a different state entirely. She might decide to travel.

The very thought of traveling to places unknown gave her a jolt of energy; however, that energy turned to fear when she realized how lonely it would be to travel without Lee, the person she loved the most in this world.

She drove around for an hour and ended up at the Northwood Cemetery where a lot of her mother's friends and relatives were buried.

And Lee.

She drove along the paved roads, past numerous headstones and monuments, around another curve to the family plot. Lee was buried between one of her cousins who had died during childhood and an elderly uncle, both on her mother's side.

Lee's father, who was still alive and in assisted living in Coshocton, wasn't able to help pay for his son's burial. Cassie and Lee didn't have a will or instructions for a funeral and burial; therefore, it was decided that Lee would be buried in Cassie's family plot in Northwood. When the time came, Cassie would be cremated and her ashes interned next to Lee's.

She should have brought flowers, but in this horrid heat, she knew she wouldn't be back to water them and they would die.

Cassie walked down the rows of tombstones and stopped at Harlon's grave. The granite marker was gone, replaced with a small rock. *I'll have to ask Grandmother what's going on. Why is his marker replaced with a rock? Is the replacement temporary or permanent? By the way, where is his military marker?*

The heat combined with this mystery of Grandfather's missing tombstone caused Cassie to expect a fainting spell. But before she broke down completely, she ran to her car, started it up, and waited for the blast of cold air from the air conditioner to revive her.

Soon enough, she started to shiver. She turned the radio on, hoping music would calm her.

As she flipped through the stations, she found only commercials and turned the radio back off.

She sat in her car and watched a haze settle among the tombstones. The ground was dry from lack of rain; the grass brown in spots. *They should turn the sprinkler system on*, she thought. *Our loved ones should be surrounded by lush green grass and flowers. Hundreds of beautiful flowers. Roses and forget-me-nots. Lilies of the valley.*

The child's grave, with the engraved name and angel beside her family-plot, always made her sad. Then she thought about Lee, also young but not a child, and grief would consume her little by little until she thought she might suffocate.

She turned the key in the ignition and drove along the road to the entrance, that was also the exit. The other two exits were gated and padlocked. She felt that her vehicle floated around curves and up hills, past monuments, statues, crypts.

Why was Grandfather's grave disturbed, the marker clearly downsized?

CHAPTER 8

"Why is Grandfather's headstone replaced with a rock?" Cassie asked that evening when she returned to the Tudor House and found Grandmother Eva sitting in a chair surrounded by twenty-five hundred feet of velvety red and white roses.

"Why?" Eva echoed, pressing the top of her wide-brimmed hat with her hand and squinting up at Cassie. "Why not? I'm having the original repaired."

Eva had been pulling weeds. In the heat of August, she preferred early morning and evening to work in the yard. It wasn't a task she particularly enjoyed, but it was therapeutic and made her feel useful. It also helped ease a back injury she suffered years ago when she fell during a rock-climbing adventure.

"The marker was chipped by the storm last winter and the death date was wrong. Remember? I couldn't cope with having the date changed so soon after the burial."

Although she was wearing tinted glasses, Eva still squinted at Cassie. "Help me stand up," she said.

Cassie took her grandmother's hand which was not a soft, feminine one, but Cassie knew that, even as a girl, Eva helped Grandfather McClure in the mines. Eva was his only child, and she believed it was her responsibility to assume the role of both daughter and son.

Cassie clutched the strap of her bag over her left shoulder and supported Grandmother with her other hand as they headed for the back porch. It was a long way to go from the front yard, where the rose gardens lined up according to color—red, pink, white and yellow—across the glorious green lawn to the back of the house, and finally, to the steps leading up to the huge screened-in porch.

Rarely did they enter the Tudor House through the front door, although the front porch and door ensemble was a marvel in itself. The door was ten feet tall and constructed of glass with a mahogany frame. There was a gold-plated lantern above it, and during this time of evening the light glowed systematically in a curtain of pale yellow all the way down the red brick landing.

The steps to the yard were made of marble. An odd contrast, the brick and marble, but Cassie had to admit the combination worked.

If nothing else, the house was innovative, a hodge-podge of masonry and a stacking of rooms, endless hallways with odd features, such as cubbyhole doors and shelves. Secret passages.

Back to the exterior: Cassie believed the house was too much for a stranger to process in one dose. She, as a family member, would glance it over and even after all these years, still feel intimidated.

Why would anyone need or want a house this big, if not to suggest excessive wealth with no shortage of backup in the bank?

She helped Grandmother up the porch steps. Grand-mother was shrinking year by year, but in the oppressive heat, she became a burden not even Cassie wanted to take on.

They inhaled deep breaths, simultaneously, and Cassie pushed open the screen door and helped Grandmother into the cool air.

"Cassie!" a male voice yelled behind her.

She was holding Grandmother upright when they turned as one. Grandmother said, "There's our dear Eric! Find out what he wants, Cassandra, while I go in and see about refreshments."

As if Grandmother had shed years off her age just by going from the outside heat to the cool air of the porch, she vanished into the kitchen, her gardening clogs clacking against tile.

"Eric," Cassie said suspiciously. "Did Grandmother call you?"

She hoped Eric hadn't forgotten the mix-up over the back gate.

"I wanted to check on you ladies," he said. He wore casual clothing: A T-shirt, blue jeans, tennis shoes. He looked roguish and enticing. A different man entirely.

But she didn't like the way he had snuck up on them.

"Sorry if I startled you. I just wanted to see if you needed anything."

"We're fine," she said.

She looked away from his mesmerizing hazel eyes. "Nice of you to drop by," she added, dismissing him.

Grandmother Eva shouted from the kitchen foyer, "Cassie! Invite him in for some pie."

"He's busy, Grandmother! He just stopped by to say hello!" There was an edge to her voice, warning Eric to take his leave.

"I'll come back another time!" Eric yelled to Eva. "Call me if you need anything!"

Cassie watched him walk away. He must have parked on the road by the orchard because he headed in that direction.

It was turning dark now, a red and orange sunset replacing purple and gray streaks. Suddenly there was a satin breeze, a whoosh through the trees.

Cassie walked across the porch into the kitchen. Grandmother was taking dishes out of the dish rack and putting them in the cupboards. "Why didn't you invite him in, Cassandra?"

Cassie chose a cookie from a plate on the counter. "Because I'm tired. What happened to pie? Did Frances make these?"

Eva had a pot of coffee on. "I decided on cookies instead. And yes, Frances probably made them. Unless she bought them somewhere."

Cassie tossed the chocolate chip cookie back onto the plate. "Then I won't risk it. That bitch needs to go! I don't trust her!"

Eva laughed. "You have quite the imagination. You really need to use it to your advantage."

"She's *shifty*," Cassie insisted. "I want to know what the noises are in the far-left of the house. I hear sounds. I'm sure you hear them too, so please don't look at me that way."

"Cassandra, let's sit down at the table and have some coffee, talk a bit."

Eva didn't wait for Cassie's consent; as was her style, she picked up two yellow-and-green coffee cups and headed for the table. "Old houses settle, Cassandra. You know that."

"Not like a stampede of cattle!"

"Sit down and drink your coffee," Eva said stiffly. "Stop exaggerating. I want to ask you what plans you have for your house. I know a realtor who knows the market *very* well. If you want me to, I'll call him and make an appointment for him to meet us at the house on Eighth."

Her grandmother and parents always referred to Cassie and Lee's home as "the house on Eighth."

Cassie didn't like the implication: to her it sounded like "the shack," or "the silly little playhouse."

She had always thought they were making fun of her accomplishments, and worse, making fun of Lee's.

Cassie said nothing and stirred cream and sugar into her coffee. For one thing, she wondered why they were drinking coffee at seven-thirty at night. Normally, Eva wouldn't touch caffeine past four o'clock.

Eva sipped from the thin cup and watched Cassie's face. *No doubt, she's scrutinizing my every move*, thought Cassie.

"I wouldn't dillydally," Eva advised. "There are things you must do."

"I'm in no hurry," Cassie told her. "So please stop pressuring me."

"You *should* be in a hurry. I'm leaving this entire estate to you when I die."

Cassie almost spat a mouthful of coffee onto the table. She clamped a napkin to her lips. "Wh-what did you say?"

"*I said*, I am leaving this house and grounds and most of my assets to you, Cassandra."

Cassie was still unable to speak clearly, even after swallowing the coffee. "W-what about Father?"

Eva nibbled on a cookie. *Like a mouse*, thought Cassie. *Or a rat*. "What about him?"

"He *is* your son. It's obvious he thinks he will inherit his parents' estate!"

"He's an imbecile," said Eva. "With certain things," she added as tears formed in Cassie's eyes. "He has problems focusing is what I mean to say, dear. True, he's brilliant at his work, his job. But he can't seem to stay on point. You did tell him to be here tomorrow night for dinner?"

Cassie nodded yes.

Eva sipped more coffee. "Good. Frances is making a pot roast and you'll be polite to her, please. Monday morning I'll call Brian O'Dea, the realtor I told you about."

"I'm not ready," Cassie said, still stunned by Eva's announcement of leaving the house and grounds to her.

"Well, *get* ready!" Eva said as she stood up to take her cup to the counter for a refill. "Time waits for no one!"

CHAPTER 9

Harlon thought, *Time waits for no one,* but he wasn't ready to ask Eva McClure to marry him. He needed her, yes. She was strong-willed and gregarious. She was energetic and motivated. What man wouldn't want to marry her . . . and acquire the lucrative McClure Coal Mine and the acres of beautiful rolling hills in Guernsey County owned by Ian McClure? Not to mention the lush, exquisite 262-acre Homestead McClure had built over the years with his own two hands.

"Oh, God no," Eva said with a laugh when Harlon asked her specifics about the homestead.

One of Eva's front teeth was slightly crooked; thus, sometimes she lisped. "Father had a lot of help building his farm. Don't let him fool you! The neighbors helped and he hired carpenters and workers, cheap."

Cheap is key, decided Harlon. Poor people will work for low wages. Wealthy people hire them to get wealthier.

Harlon was tired of scraping by. Although he had a degree in geology and was sought after for surveying and mapping jobs in the area, he never seemed to have enough money for the things he wanted and the land he hoped to invest in.

Yes, there were characteristics about Eva he would change if he could, for instance her know-it-all attitude, her dismissal of the needy and uneducated, and her impatience with people who took too much time thinking over a problem before acting on it.

Where she got such a stringent disposition, he couldn't say. Her father was a powerful man but he never argued. McClure knew what he wanted and would either get his way or walk away. Eva's mother, Lorraine, was polite as well. However, she was animated and spirited and graceful in fashion and speech.

Lorraine had porcelain-looking skin and long dark hair that had turned partially gray by the time Harlon met her. Her eyelashes were thick, like a child's. She was thinner than her daughter, Eva, and she was feminine physically, whereas Eva, although attractive, was nothing to rave about.

Except for her smile. Eva had the most enchanting smile Harlon had ever seen and the crooked left front tooth made her even more irresistible.

• • •

Harlon took Eva to a dinner party at the country club hosted by her parents' best friends, the Jennings. Although he couldn't afford it, he rented a tuxedo for the occasion. Eva wore a light purple dress, the straps slightly off her shoulders, with a black belt cinched at the waist. The dress was silk and fell to the top of black shoes, with rhinestones down both sides of the heels. She wore a strand of pearls around her neck and a pearl on each earlobe.

"You look … magnificent," Harlon said.

"You're surprised?" Eva asked, her eyes wide.

She was disappointed in him, he could tell.

It seemed she would go back and forth: one day happy to see him, the next day treating him like he worked for *her*, not her father.

Harlon reached out to take her elbow and lead the way. "Let's find a table."

"I'd rather dance," she said.

Then she vanished into the crowd.

After she left him that night, he knew, even if he could convince her to marry him, she would always *vanish into the crowd*.

Nonetheless, he wanted her money and her influence. He needed the backing of Ian McClure.

Harlon wandered through the dancing couples to an open bar, ordered a whiskey sour, then moved among the dancers yet again and ended up standing at the table with the McClures and Jennings. The two couples reeked of alcohol and money.

It was so exhilarating, Harlon almost collapsed. He could feel his adoration for Eva oozing from his eyes and ears, and he was embarrassed by his own transparency.

Mrs. Jennings—he thought her name was Mavis—chattered away and laughed so hard even the band leader turned to see what the commotion was about.

Ian McClure, however, was quite somber, nursing a glass of brandy, red in color. "Harlon," he said in his calm manner. "Have a seat. Evie is around here somewhere."

"Eva is my date," Harlon informed them.

Eva *his* date? He could tell Lorraine was surprised to hear this when her long eyelashes lifted and her lips pinched as if to say, *You poor thing. You're no match for our spirited Eva!*

"Your— *date?*" Ian asked as if he had meant to say, "Are you out of your mind, boy?"

Harlon pulled a small box from his tuxedo jacket pocket, opened it, and showed them a ring with a tiny ruby stone.

Ian turned to Lorraine and chuckled. He was a heavyset man, and his waist shook the table with all the humor he apparently felt.

Somehow, Harlon hadn't expected this reaction from Ian McClure.

"Congratulations!" shouted Mr. Jennings. He rolled his eyes at the McClures. "And good luck to you, sonny!" When *he* laughed, the ladies clucked. Lorraine, who Harlon had believed to be so polite, started laughing uncontrollably, spilling wine on the white tablecloth.

And didn't seem to care.

Harlon could tell that *no one* cared.

Instead of searching for Eva, Harlon decided to leave and discuss the proposal with her in the morning at the mine.

He walked back to the bar to put his empty glass down on the surface. A man in a dark pinstriped suit was watching him. The man had a pointed face with a skinny black moustache above his thick lips. He smiled at Harlon with teeth that looked like identical squares of ivory.

He came toward Harlon. "Harold Larrabee," he said, smiling and smelling of strong cologne. "I'm the owner here."

"Hello," said Harlon.

Harlon hesitated to make conversation, mostly because he was anxious to leave the premises before he bumped into Eva again.

"Would you like another drink?" asked Harold Larrabee in a rather high voice. "It's on the house, of course."

"No thanks," said Harlon. "I'm leaving. I've an early morning at work."

"Oh, well," said Larrabee, looking dumbstruck. "It's only nine o'clock!"

"Thank you anyway," said Harlon. He was irritated with the stranger's persistence. He didn't like being approached as if he were *anyone's* darling. There was something about this man he didn't like, and something about him he liked too much.

Harlon could feel Harold Larrabee watching him walk across the dance floor and out the front door.

CHAPTER 10

Cassie wasn't looking forward to seeing her parents at dinner. She got up early, had coffee and toast with Eva, and left the kitchen as soon as Frances arrived.

Frances was expected to clean the living room, sitting room, and the dining room where they would eat. She was to make dinner: roast beef, rolls, two salads, and a dessert of double-layer cherry cheesecake. "Roy's favorite," said Grandmother.

Cassie stayed in her room, researching real estate companies on the internet. She would find her own agent. Grandmother would choose someone old and stodgy anyway, not a person close to Cassie's age who might relate to her needs.

First, she wanted an idea of what her house was worth. She needed to know if an agent would suggest changes or if she could sell as is. She didn't want to put money into repairing the garage roof that leaked or the shower with mold in the corner. She was hoping to get a good price with repairs pending.

Her house on Eighth Avenue was near the grade school and high school, two selling points. Her street was within walking distance to the public park and swimming pool; there was a bus stop at the corner of her street and every couple of hours a transit bus would pick up people who didn't drive or wish to. Another selling point, she decided.

She made her bed and straightened the dresser drawers. She wanted her clothes ready to wear. She went to the walk-in closet and separated her blouses and dresses that were on hangers. When she found the back wall, she pushed on it and traced her fingers along the area, back and forth, until she found an indented outline of a rectangle. But this small area, the size of a three-foot-by-two-foot window, had been sealed shut.

Cassie was about to push the wall, but there was a knock on the bedroom door.

She backed out of the closet. "Yes? Who is it?"

"It's Frances," came a serrated voice. "Your grand-mother says your parents are here and dinner is ready."

That shrewd crow, thought Cassie. *She's been spying on me.*

• • •

Cassie could smell roast beef as soon as she stepped off the stairway. Odd that she couldn't smell dinner cooking throughout the house until she got closer to the dining room. She was beginning to get suspicious about a lot more than secret doorways.

She was wearing blue shorts, a red, short-sleeved blouse, and sandals. Obviously underdressed: her mother had on dark-green linen pants and a sleeveless blouse ensemble, white sandals, and a necklace made of orange and clear rhinestones. Her hair had been styled into a sleek bob with blonde highlights.

When Rachel smiled at Cassie, her white teeth gleamed. There was a deep dimple at the right side of her glossy lips. Cassie thought, *What a beautiful woman, my mother.*

Roy was a different matter. He had on shorts that were too tight, showing blobs of who knows what, and consequently, he looked ridiculously out of place at Grandmother's dinner table. He also wore a flamboyant red-and-yellow Hawaiian shirt. Cassie couldn't tell: was it a blouse? A T-shirt beneath a halter top? Roy was standing at the sideboard behind the table, serving himself from a decanter of bourbon. There was also a coffee maker set up and sputtering, next to two bottles of wine.

He turned when Cassie entered the room and lifted his glass in a toast.

"There's my girl," he said. "We've been waiting dinner on you!"

And drinking while waiting, she thought when she noticed even Grandmother was smiling-stupidly. "Sit down, dear," Grandmother said. "Would you like a cocktail before we eat?"

"No, thank you," said Cassie.

Cassie sat down beside her mother, who was doused in sweet-smelling perfume. Cassie wanted to move away from her, the scent was so strong, but she stayed put.

Grandmother wore a plain, navy-blue pantsuit. She did something to her hair as well but it wasn't professionally worked-over; it was flipped around her head and held in place with a pink bandana. *What the hell*, thought Cassie. *She looks .... demented.*

Rachel grabbed Cassie's hand and squeezed. "Good to see you, honey," she said. "It's been a while."

"Good to see you too, Mother," Cassie lied. "I just missed you the other day when I came over to visit Father."

"Yes, he told me you were there. And he told me *why* you were there."

"Oh my," said Grandmother, rotating her eyes to the ceiling fan above.

It's absurd, thought Cassie, *the way Grandmother opens her mouth and shakes her head at the ceiling. As if the fan knows what Mother had meant.*

"I wanted to talk to him about my investments," continued Cassie. "I want to—"

Out of nowhere came Frances carrying a platter of sliced roast beef. She made a spectacle of herself, weaving throughout the room, pushing a chair aside with her hip so abruptly her left sandal caught on the gray Oriental carpet. "Oh, dammit to hell!" she shouted.

"Frances!" yelled Grandmother.

No one offered to get up and help her.

Frances put the platter down in front of Eva, but Eva looked at her with a childish pursing of her lips. "Thank you, Frances," she said, her eyelids batting. "Bring in the salads and potatoes and then you can leave."

Frances retreated back to the kitchen. "We'll continue talking after *she* leaves," said Grandmother conspiratorially, going for her wineglass and another sip.

Frances made two more trips back and forth from the kitchen. "Anything else?" she asked hastily. "Before I leave?"

"We've got it, thank you, Frances," Eva said softly.

Frances turned on her heel and disappeared.

They passed the platter of meat down the table, then started on the salad bowls and the potatoes. Next came the butter dish and the gravy boat. There was a clatter of silverware, the sloshing of wine poured into glasses, over and over again.

Ten minutes passed. The ceiling fan spinned. The porch door slammed shut behind Frances.

"Well, then, Roy," said Eva after wiping her mouth with a napkin. "Tell Cassie what you told me last week."

Rachel put her fork down on her plate and lowered her hands under the table. She looked around the meticulously decorated room and over at her wealthy mother-in-law.

One by one, they stared at Roy, who was chewing. He put another forkful of potatoes into his mouth, chewed and chewed, and finally washed it down with bourbon before looking at Cassie and saying, "I'm sorry, Cassandra. Very sorry to tell you this. But I sold your stocks a year ago and spent all the money."

CHAPTER 11

Cassie got up from the dinner table, threw her napkin down on the chair, and left the room. She wanted to outrun a panic attack, plain and simple. She realized two things. One: her father had lied to her all these years by saying the stocks were hers when obviously they weren't, otherwise, he wouldn't have been able to cash them in. Two: She was broke and had no choice. She would definitely need to sell her house.

Cassie heard their voices behind her as she headed for upstairs. She would stay in her bedroom until they left.

On second thought, she'd get her handbag, run back down the stairway, zip past them in the hallway, through the kitchen, and out the back door.

She ran up the stairs so fast she thought she was going to faint and fall back to the first floor. That would solve her problems. She would surely break her neck.

Let them live with my death!

"Cassie!" yelled Grandmother.

She kept running, running … up the last six steps and turned right to her bedroom. Out of breath, she opened the door, closed it behind her. Although she was still grieving over Lee, she could clearly see that her father was failing.

He has taken to drinking, she decided, a condition she did not recall when she was a child and lived with her parents. *Drinking himself to death and spending everyone's money!*

Thinking back, her childhood was rich with activities: camping, dance classes, piano lessons, summers with Grandmother Eva, trips to the Southwest, East Coast, Italy, and France. She excelled in school. She won awards. She was a member of the student council and graduated with honors.

Her childhood and teen years were invigorating and satisfying.

Her parents would go to parties, but they *never* came home drunk.

Now she clearly understood why her father was deteriorating. *He has lost his enthusiasm for life,* she thought. *He's falling apart, piece by piece.*

But that didn't give him the right to spend her savings.

"Cassie," said Grandmother at the door. "Your father wants to speak with you."

Cassie had nothing more to say, to any of them. Instead, she was entranced by the scene in the yard below. The sunset behind the maple and pine trees had faded to orange and red hues of color and as she pulled the curtain farther to the left, she saw Eric. He was clearing brush, tugging and pulling and piling branches next to a fence that marked off the recently mowed yard.

He wore a long-sleeved shirt, jeans and work boots. He must be devoted to Grandmother Eva, Cassie thought, working *this* hard for her.

She looked for her handbag and remembered she had hidden it inside the walk-in closet, on the third shelf to the left, tucked behind a stack of sweaters.

She didn't trust Frances, or whoever else lurked the hallways of this *mausoleum*, as her father called Eva's mansion.

So, she listened at the top of the stairway until she was satisfied that Grandmother was gone; hopefully, sending Cassie's parents off with cheesecake to go.

The air-conditioning clicked back on as she moved down the staircase. She knew there was a door by the sitting room. They called it a sitting room, but it was a library with a couch, a desk, three rocking chairs, and a fireplace rarely lit.

There were hundreds of books, old and new, on shelves built into the walls. "The reproduction of the actual sitting room in my parents' house where Harlon and I talked before our Christmas Eve wedding," Eva had told her.

The door to outside was next to this room and always locked—an emergency exit of sorts. If Cassie remembered correctly, this door was between the library and a small bathroom. The last time she used the bathroom, she was eleven and had been playing outside with three of her friends.

The bathroom smelled of stagnant air, of lingering cigarette smoke and mold. There was a sink with a mirror above it, a toilet, and a cabinet as tall as the ceiling. The walls were a dingy green.

As Cassie recalled the warm summer days of her childhood and early teens, she tried once again to come up with memories of Grandfather Harlon.

Did he smoke?

Cassie found the exit door; there were two bolts and a chain locking it. She switched the bolts and slid the chain. She opened the door to dead flies and cobwebs stuck against the outer glass door.

There were three cement steps and a watering hose attached to a plastic holder. She shut both doors behind her, thinking the doors would just have to remain unlocked until she returned.

She followed the buzz of a chainsaw over to where Eric was cleaning up debris, branches, and pieces of bark. She moved along the side of the house but stopped when she saw that a window near the lower end of the brick exterior was cracked open.

This must be a mistake; no one would leave a window open to the basement of the house. She wanted to close it but decided to ask Eric about it first.

Before she got to him, he turned off the saw and began piling branches into a heap near the glider swing.

"Hi, Eric," she said, holding her bag close to her side. "What are you doing here this time of evening?"

He looked at her as if he had expected her to show up. "I work all day at the shop, so I try to come here in the evenings to help with the yard work. If your gramma needs me."

"I see. Do you happen to know why one of the basement windows is open?"

"No, unless she wanted it aired out." Cassie watched him pick up several more branches before he took off his gloves and stuffed them in the pocket of his jeans. "Show me," he said.

Cassie backtracked through the yard, Eric following. He brushed dirt off his shirt as he walked behind her.

"That's strange," he said, studying the window. "This is the window she had me seal shut a couple of weeks ago."

"I'm going to go back in the house and ask her," said Cassie. More and more she felt uncomfortable living here, but more and more she needed to know why.

"Don't do that!" he said. "Let me look around first."

"It shouldn't be open. Squirrels can get in, and rain! There must be humidifiers in the basement and cellar. There's no need to keep a window open."

"You're right," he said. "That's why she wanted me to seal it up. Now it's open again."

"I think we should go inside and down to the basement so we can figure out what's going on. Come this way." She led him toward the same side door she had exited five minutes earlier.

She opened the screen door, then she opened the heavier wooden door and they stepped into the cool hallway. "Shut the doors behind you," she said. "Bolt and chain the last one."

They walked down the hallway, but Cassie couldn't remember which way to turn. Was the basement door to the left off the kitchen? Below the stairway to the second floor?

"There's another stairway," said Eric. "It's toward the back of the house, off the spare bedroom she keeps for storage. Sometimes she sleeps in there too. Or so she says."

Cassie couldn't believe she didn't know there was another stairway to the second floor and *he* did.

"I had no idea there was another stairway," she said.

She wondered if he was thinking the same thing . . . that something vital is off with her family's communication.

They moved down the hallway, single file. Obviously, this section of the house wasn't used much, or not at all, judging by the dust and cobwebs.

"The door's over here." Eric walked up to a door and turned the knob. Cassie thought for sure it would be locked, but it wasn't. He went through the door.

"Follow close behind me," he said. "I've only been down here once with your gramma and my dad. I was just a kid, probably about seven."

Cassie stayed right behind him, feeling his body heat mixed with the musty air. There was a stairway near the lower tier and there was also a steep stairway going upward.

"And that goes where?" she asked in a whisper.

"I guess to the attic. I've never been up there, but your gramma said there's an attic, so that must be it."

As they moved down the stairway, Cassie pressed up against Eric's back. He didn't seem to mind, but she was afraid of the dark and even more afraid they might fall down the steps.

He didn't have a flashlight and used his foot to feel the way. Halfway down the steps, he flipped a light switch.

"I knew there was a light," he said. "If not, we would have to turn back for a flashlight."

But the light was too dim and she clutched him even harder, encumbered by the bag slung over her shoulder, the weight of it wedged between her chest and his back. She thought the stairway would never end although finally, they came to the last step.

Surprisingly, the basement interior wasn't damp; in fact, it had a cement floor with rugs scattered about, and there were two humidifiers, both humming.

There were several rectangular windows, all closed except for the window she noticed was open. The window Eric claimed Eva told him to seal shut from the outside.

Cassie became intrigued when she saw hundreds of boxes stacked along three walls of the interior. There were clothes wrapped in plastic and hanging from racks. There were shelves of smaller boxes and crates lined up and stacked, and lamps, hats, shoeboxes, and an assortment of knickknacks and vases.

Next to a bookshelf, she saw Grandmother's shotgun, the very gun Grandmother kept in her bedroom. *Why was the shotgun here? Who took it from Grandmother's room and left it down here?*

But she didn't mention it to Eric.

As she looked around, Eric shut the window and turned the latch to lock it.

Cassie wanted answers. She wanted details. She wanted to go through every box, open all the wooden chests and find out what they held within. "What do you make of this, Eric?"

"I don't know but she sure keeps a lot of junk."

"I would love to go through it all," Cassie admitted. "She probably kept a lot of vintage dresses and jewelry. Maybe some valuable artwork."

Cassie walked over to a cedar chest. There was a skeleton key in the lock, but the lid was unlocked. Her eyes widened at the treasure inside. There was a wooden separation, thus two sides to the chest. One side held thin boxes, the other side pockets of jewelry—gold and silver chains, diamonds, and gemstone rings and bracelets. She found a large manila envelope that had *Harlon's Military Records* scribbled on it. She wanted to take the envelope to study it but got distracted. "Look at this!" She reached down to an opened box of coins. Then she saw a stack of one-hundred-dollar bills. Right beside the stack—tied with blue ribbon—was another stack of bills and two more. Next, she found an old book and inside the cover was looping handwriting she recognized as Eva's: *Evalyn Brigid McClure.*

"Who's down there?" someone shouted from the top of the stairs.

CHAPTER 12

Three months had passed since the country club incident and now marrying Eva was all Harlon could think about. He was thirty-nine years old. He wanted to settle down and start a family. He made a good living as a surveyor, but he wanted more.

He wanted Eva.

Eva was very independent and didn't pay attention to him; therefore, Harlon knew he would have to take drastic measures. He had asked her to the dance at the country club and she accepted, but disappeared into the crowd almost as soon as they walked through the doors.

He knew he could never *control* her. He only wanted legal access to her bank accounts. And her trust fund.

"Mr. McClure," Harlon said one day as he entered McClure's drafty office at the mines. He had to wait for McClure to finish writing in the daily ledger. As always in Ian McClure's presence, Harlon started to sweat.

McClure dropped the pen and leaned back in his leather chair. "Yes, Hall?" he said with an edge to his voice. He clasped his hands over a tight vest and waited. He had gained weight, even though he strolled the grounds daily, and other than office work, he wasn't one to sit idle.

"I need some advice on dating your daughter. I want to get to know her, you see. And she . . ." Harlon did his best not to stammer. He cleared his throat. "She seems not to want anything to do with me."

"It's just her nature," said McClure without raising or lowering his voice. "I doubt she's interested in being tied down."

"I really like and admire her," Harlon explained. "I want to take her out to dinner. Get to know her—"

McClure interrupted. "She was in a relationship five years ago. The man proposed. They made wedding plans but for some reason, he changed his mind and left town." McClure spoke so matter-of-factly; Harlon knew there was no way he could make any of this up. "I suspect she's gun-shy," McClure added hastily, picking up his pen and leaning forward to continue his work. "Just ask her out, Hall," he said by way of ending the conversation. "And good luck to you on *that!*"

Harlon left McClure's office. Three days passed before he saw her again in town, at a bank of all places. He had withdrawn enough cash from his savings to buy groceries and pay the rent. He was living in an apartment building in the middle of town. It was a convenient location and semi-luxurious, but Harlon knew he could do better.

Eva was waiting in line. She wore a tan skirt with a matching jacket, a fur hat (probably mink to match the collar of her jacket, he thought), gold bracelets, and a gold chain around her neck.

Where, he wondered, *is she going dressed to the hilt?*

He stood near one of the office cubicles and watched her chat with the teller while conducting business. No cash exchanged hands. She was depositing checks. This much he could see from afar. Hearing what was being said between Eva and the teller was a different matter.

She turned, slid around the stout woman standing behind her in line, and headed towards the exit.

He stepped directly in front of her. "Eva!" He said, sounding surprised to see her. "How nice to run into you!"

She lifted her head to stare him down. He noticed that the only makeup she wore was peach-colored blush and lipstick to match. "I'm in a hurry, Harlon."

"I was wondering if you'd like to have lunch with me."

She consulted her diamond-studded wristwatch. "It's three o'clock." She shook her head at such audacity. *No one eats lunch at three o'clock*, he imagined her thinking.

"I'm sorry," she said. "I have errands to run."

"Then dinner this evening at seven? Spencer's?"

His thoughts buzzed forward to the perfect reason: "I have a business proposal I'd like to discuss with you before bringing it up with Mr. McClure. I mean—your father."

Her lips pressed together before she said, "Fine. Seven at Spencer's."

He was so surprised she accepted his invitation for dinner, he almost fell backwards.

She rushed to the front door and disappeared.

He stood completely stunned. He had to get himself together, finish up an errand, and go back to his apartment in time to re-dress for dinner.

"Hello again!" He turned, still dazed by Eva's acceptance to have dinner with him, and found the owner of the country club, Harold Larrabee. "I thought that was you!" said Larrabee. "I was in the back discussing a renovation project with Camden. You know Milton Camden?"

Harlon had heard of Milton Camden, the bank president, but he didn't *know* him.

He pretended otherwise. "Yes, I know Milton. Or rather, my boss, Ian McClure, does. Quite well."

"You work for Ian McClure? The coal mine baron?" Larrabee asked, incredulous.

"That's the one. Well, I don't work for him per se; I survey for his company."

"He's quite the character!" said Larrabee. "He's somewhat of an icon around these parts. Started his company from nothing; a hard worker, that one. And a lot of luck with finding locations. He bought a stretch of land near National Mine, more in Center Township, discovered coal on both surfaces. Six months later, he found coal veins for literally miles below!" When Larrabee became excited, which Harlon noticed was often, his pencil moustache quivered. He was tall and lanky and he had watery-brown eyes and brown hair. His hair was pressed flat against his head, tapered short around his ears.

It was troubling to Harlon the way he looked into Harlon's eyes. Deeply. Wanting something. "Would you care to join me for a drink?" Harold asked. "I'm celebrating a deal I'm about to finalize. You see, I own the club but I'm also a developer. I'm about to build a new hotel north of Zanesville. Please join me," he pleaded. "Just one drink?"

Harlon nodded and followed him out the door of the bank and across the street to the tavern. Harold quickly selected a table near a painting of a meadow with pine trees, the colors green and brown.

He pulled a chair out for Harlon, acting like the host he was known for. He was so rich; he could do and be whomever he pleased.

"Let's start with champagne!" Harold said enthusiastically. The waiter approached their table and Harold ordered a bottle of champagne.

"Tell me all about yourself, Harlon," Harold said, eyes sparkling. "I want to know *everything* about you."

• • •

Harlon was late for dinner. Eva was already at Spencer's, sitting at a table in front of the bay window. "I was about to leave," she said, vexed. "It's seven thirty, Harlon. I tell you; I was just about to leave when I saw you come through the front door!"

"I'm so sorry," Harlon said.

He adjusted his tie and attempted to put his hand over hers, but she pulled her hand away.

"I help my father all day with his business and also help Mother with the house and her charity events," Eva said in no uncertain terms. "I don't have time for people who can't stick to agreements. You said seven. I was here precisely at seven."

"I was delayed with a schedule problem for work," he offered, thinking she would understand a work-related dispute. "It's very frustrating trying to deal with people who aren't reliable!"

Wrong thing to say, he realized when Eva frowned.

"Anyway, I'm here now!" he said. "I see you've ordered coffee?"

"Yes, I don't drink except for occasionally at parties. I don't like alcohol. I prefer coffee."

"Very good." He scanned down the menu. "What to have, what to have," he said pleasantly.

"Harlon!" Eva snapped her fingers to get his attention. "You have a scratch near your mouth. It's bleeding."

Harlon touched the side of his mouth. He thought about Harold sucking and chewing. Harold smelling of exotic spices.

He could smell Harold now and hoped Eva would assume the fragrance was originally on *him*, not transplanted from someone else.

But Harlon knew the lingering scent was Harold's heady cologne and deodorant combined. Harold's peppermint breath. Harold's double bed in Harold's suite in one of Harold's hotels.

Harold's tongue against his bare skin.

Harlon tugged at the collar of his white shirt. He knew he was sweating, and God help him if Eva noticed. "I scratched myself," he said. "Somehow. My goodness!" He laughed and dabbed at the spot of blood with his napkin. "I'm a reckless one!"

He hoped she would laugh, grin, make light of his comment in some noncommittal way. But she stared. She studied. She barely touched her coffee.

She knows, he decided.

CHAPTER 13

Cassie thought she was going to faint. She grabbed Eric's arm, but the light at the top of the stairway was on and there was no way around it; they were caught.

Cassie took charge as Eric closed the lid to the cedar chest.

"It's me! Cassie!" she yelled upward. "I found this by accident and decided to check it out. I need space to store some of my things from the house."

There were footsteps descending the stairway. They held their breath and waited to see who it was, but Cassie already knew: Frances.

Frances grabbed the banister railing with both hands. "You've done it now!" she said, her head shaking. "No one is supposed to be down here!"

"You know, Frances," Cassie shouted. "This is my grandmother's home, not yours! I can check out the entire place, room by room, if I want! I have a right to it! You don't!"

"Fine!" Frances yelled from her position in the middle of the stairway. "But don't do any snooping!"

"Why should you care?" Cassie yelled back. "What business is it of yours?"

Eric was going to say something in Cassie's defense but Cassie put a finger to her lips to silence him. Better for Frances to think Cassie was alone. Less suspicion.

Besides, Eric was Grandmother's right-hand man and Cassie wanted to keep it that way.

"Don't bother running to Grandmother to tell her you found me down here, Frances!" Cassie shouted. "I plan to talk to her today about storing some of my furniture here. From now on, you stay out of things between my grandmother and me. Understand?"

"You little brat!" Frances yelled from above. "You have no idea what you're getting into! No damned idea!"

Cassie heard her take her leave in a flutter of grunts and swear words.

Finally, she was gone.

"That's interesting," Eric whispered. "What did she mean by 'you have no idea?'"

"She's just a troublemaker. I'm coming back here later. I want to check this out some more." Cassie opened the lid to the cedar chest and grabbed a wad of bills. She shoved the money into her bag.

Endorphins made her dizzy, seduced her with plans for all the jewelry and cash they had found.

She realized Eric didn't approve of her taking the cash. He was shaking his head and walking towards the stairway. She went back to the chest, lifted the lid, and returned the thick stack of bills. "Dammit," she said.

• • •

She had no intention of telling Grandmother Eva about Frances catching them in the hidden basement. She wanted to see what Frances would do: tell Grandmother, or take Cassie's threat seriously and believe Cassie would ask about storing some of her items down there.

Eva caught Cassie off guard when Cassie walked into the dining room later that evening to join her for supper. Frances was nowhere to be found. Cassie knew this for a fact because the kitchen was empty, and she could tell by the snack tray of cheese, crackers, and a variety of fruit that Eva had prepared the meal herself.

"There you are," said Eva, smiling. "Let's have a light supper and do some catching up. How far along are you with sorting through items on Eighth?"

Cassie sat across from Eva and reached for a cracker and a wedge of Colby cheese. "I put that aside. I'm still reeling from Father's announcement that he sold all my stock."

"Yes," Eva said sadly. "Things happen. It's very unfortunate that he resorted to cashing in your savings. A pity you were only listed as beneficiary. I'm afraid Roy is losing ground with his senses."

The way Grandmother suggested Roy was losing his mind upset Cassie. Grandmother's attitude was so "come what may" and she seemed absolutely resigned to the fact that her son was ill. "He used to be reliable," Eva continued, nibbling on an apple slice. "So sharp." She looked over Cassie's shoulder absent-mindedly and tsk-tsked—her tongue clicking against the roof of her mouth.

Cassie wanted to ask about the stairway to the blocked off area of the basement, but something told her not to bring it up. Knowing about the basement would stay a secret, and besides, Cassie hadn't decided what to do about the cache of jewelry, letters, books, and of course, the bundles of money.

"We have an appointment this evening with the real estate agent I told you about. Brian O'Dea," Eva said after drinking half a glass of wine. "We meet him at his office at seven-thirty."

Cassie was in the middle of chewing two grapes at once. She swallowed and paused. "I didn't say I was ready to meet with a realtor," she said, taken aback by Eva drinking wine and making critical decisions for her. "I haven't decided what to do with the furniture yet."

"You can talk with Brian anyway," said Eva, seemingly unperturbed by Cassie's lack of motivation. "He can give you the lowdown on the housing market. Sell that house and buy a smaller one, as soon as possible."

Cassie sipped some water. She decided it might be a good idea to discuss selling her house with an expert. She wanted to find out if she could sell the house with its current flaws, especially now that she knew she didn't have much money to invest in repair work.

"I want to change clothes and freshen up," Cassie said abruptly, and pushed her chair back to stand up.

"I'll do the same," said Eva. "You'll have to drive. I've had too much wine."

And yet, she had always claimed to hate alcohol, thought Cassie.

• • •

Cassie changed into a blue blouse and navy-blue denim capris. She brushed her blonde-brown hair until it shined and secured it to the back of her head with silver barrettes.

She had lost at least ten pounds this summer due to the extreme heat and very little appetite. The diamond engagement ring Lee had given her was too big for her finger now, so she took the ring off and put it in her jewelry box.

She reclined on the back porch, enjoying the cool air while waiting for Eva. The air conditioner motor was clanging and wheezing as if overworked. *Good,* she thought. *An excuse to call Eric.*

Why is Grandmother taking so long?

Cassie checked her watch. She had only been waiting fifteen minutes but it felt more like a half hour. *If Grandmother is plastered*, thought Cassie, *she might have fallen. She might have passed out in the upstairs hallway.*

Cassie went back into the house, disgusted that she had to check, just because Grandmother had too much wine. Years ago, Grandmother told Cassie she wouldn't chance the idea of alcohol impairing her senses.

Halfway up the stairs, Cassie heard Grandmother's voice. And also, a man's voice? It wasn't Frances's and it surely wasn't Eric's.

Cassie took two more steps and gasped when Grandmother suddenly appeared, her face deformed with rage and her purse swinging like a weapon, should anyone or anything get in her way.

"Cassandra!" she said, her other hand lifting to her chest. "You startled me!"

Grandmother looked so angry, Cassie thought she was going to jump off the top step and throttle her.

"Do *not*," she said, sucking in icy breaths, "sneak up on me like that *ever* again!"

Cassie was dumbstruck by the command, from Grandmother, no less, but Cassie didn't defend herself and she certainly didn't reveal that she heard voices—one Grandmother's, the other a man's.

Cassie went back down the stairway, Grandmother Eva following. Cassie held the swinging kitchen door open for her and the porch door too. They walked in silence to the garage where Cassie had parked her car.

Cassie clicked the locks, opened the passenger side for Eva, and waited for her to slide onto the leather seat and pull the door shut.

After Cassie backed out and turned down the long driveway, she said, "I hope this doesn't take long. I want to go to bed early tonight."

As if small talk was all that was left between them.

"Fair enough, Casandra," said Eva. "I just think it is a good idea to meet with Brian to give you an idea of the current market. Do your research. *Always* do your research!"

Cassie turned the air conditioner down as she steered the Impala along the curves and hills towards the highway. "That's fine," she said. "But from now on, I'll make my own appointments."

• • •

Brian O'Dea's office was in two-story building with another realty company, a bank, and ten apartments. Thankfully, his office, Sunny Realty, was on the first floor, the second door from the entrance.

Although it was 7:20 in the evening, the heat was unrelenting. They navigated the four cement steps to the front door, Eva taking forever, even with Cassie's help.

Brian was right on the other side of the door and opened it, lifting Cassie's burden by sliding his hand under Eva's elbow and directing them to two cushioned chairs.

He deposited them, one at a time, and settled into the chair behind his desk.

"Good to see you again, Mrs. Hall," he said to Eva. He jumped up and held out a hand for Cassie to shake. "And you must be Cassandra," he said cheerfully.

"Call me Cassie," she said.

Brian wore black trousers and a gray dress shirt, no tie. He had on black leather shoes. He looked sharp and smelled good too, with a touch of minty aftershave.

His skin was smooth overall and his nose was a perfect size and shape to match the contours of his facial structure. He had beautiful brown eyes and she could tell his hair was professionally cut and styled, but she couldn't tell if the blonde blending through the brown was natural or highlighted.

Eva said briskly, "As you know, Cassandra wants to put her house on Eighth Avenue on the market as soon as possible." Cassie turned to glare at her. Ignoring Cassie's warning, Eva said, "Isn't that right, Cassandra?"

Cassie's eyes were back on Brian. "Not exactly. I'm *thinking* about it."

"Well, thinking and doing are two different animals," said Eva, a sharp stab to her voice. "I *think* we decided it's time for a change."

"You decided, Grandmother," said Cassie.

Brian shifted in his chair. "It doesn't hurt to look around," he told Cassie. "For when you *are* ready. If ever."

"My husband died two years ago," said Cassie. "We picked the house out together and lived there for almost four years. I'm not quite ready to get rid of it." The last of her speech was directed to Eva. She felt her face heat up and knew that if she wasn't careful, tears would fall.

Brian jumped out of his chair again, holding out a tissue. "Thank you," she whispered, impressed by his compassion.

"If you like, I can meet you sometime this week and take a look at it," he said gently, as if his words were made of cotton and he didn't want them torn. *"If* you're ready."

Eva was silent. She looked around the room, apparently inspecting the awards Sunny Realty Company—and Brian—had received.

Cassie said, "I don't know," which prompted Eva to roll her eyes. "I suppose we could meet and go through it, get some ideas."

"That's fine," he said. "Why don't you go home and think about it some more. I'll call you midweek."

Cassie nodded.

"Here's my card." He pulled out a business card, turned it over, and scribbled on the back. "This is my private number. Call me anytime." He handed the card to her over the top of his desk.

Eva, however, clicked her tongue against the roof of her mouth and shot Brian an "I told you so" look. Whereas Cassie noticed, he didn't acknowledge her *code.*

He was looking at Cassie as if he understood her perspective all too well.

"Thank you," said Cassie. "You ready to go, Grand-mother?"

Cassie stood up, looked down at Eva, and proceeded to pull Eva out of the chair.

"Thank you for your time, Brian," Eva said. "We'll be in touch."

"No problem, ladies!" Brian stood up too. "It's been a pleasure."

Outside, as they walked down the steps to the sidewalk, Eva said, "Cassandra, dear. What's gotten into you? Don't you want to start over? Don't you think it's time to stop grieving and move on?"

"I don't know," Cassie whimpered. "I miss Lee so much. If I give up the house, I have nothing left of him."

Eva stopped and pulled Cassie to her. "Now you listen to me," she said. "I know your husband died far too young and you didn't have enough time together, but life goes on. Do you think I gave a damn about anything after your grandfather died or after *my father* died? No indeed. But my theory is: we were left behind for a reason. And if you don't get a hold of yourself and move on, what kind of tribute is that to Lee? What, if anything, does giving up say about *you*, Cassandra?"

"But I loved him so much," Cassie muttered, wiping her nose with the tissue.

"Love!" spat Eva. "Love!" she spat again. "Are you *that* naïve!"

"What do you mean?" Cassie cried. "You're calling me naïve because I loved my husband and I miss him? Didn't you love Grandfather Harlon?"

Eva shook her head and walked onward.

"Grandmother!" Cassie shouted after her.

Eva turned to stare at her granddaughter. "Love him?" she asked, shaking her head as if she couldn't believe Cassie would even ask such a question. "I barely knew the son of a bitch."

Chapter 14

E va was tired of waiting at the coffee shop for Harlon. She was on her second cup of coffee and had ordered a cinnamon roll, now half-eaten.

I detest people who can't be on time, she thought, her temperature rising. *Seems to me this Harlon character is always late. Why did I agree to meet him again?*

She left the coffee shop and went to the five-and-dime to purchase cough drops and Kleenex. It was March. Due to spending a lot of time outside in the blustery weather helping her father collect data on the mining progress—the housing updates and attendance records of the miners overall—she was getting a sore throat and a horrific earache.

For days on end she had studied and reflected on how the union helped the workers acquire better living conditions in the mining towns. Quite frequently, against her father's wishes, upgraded safety regulations were carried out, providing reasonable hours and higher pay. She would never tell Father, but she agreed with the upgrades.

The newer, safer equipment included improved drag-lines and the stronger, well-built coal docks over the railroad tracks, she believed, were a godsend. Therefore, in the present time, early 1960s, Eva knew the working conditions were better and safer. Her previous mindset that the workers were only steps to her success and wealth had changed. Fair was fair, and using human lives to build her father's empire was wrong.

He was rich enough.

When she arrived back at the office, there was a bouquet of red roses waiting for her on her father's desk where she typed up documents and letters. She was curious about the sender, never thinking that maybe the arrangement was from Harlon Hall. But it was. The card read: *I'm sorry. Affectionately, Harlon.*

She decided to go home for the day. She was about to lock the door behind her, but went back into the office to collect the bouquet. She would put the roses in a vase of water at home, if nothing else.

• • •

After dinner, as Eva was sipping tea in her father's study with both of her parents, she mentioned Harlon. "I wonder, Father, if you would please hire someone else to survey the locations."

Ian was puffing on a cigar and reading a page of the newspaper. He always read the paper this way: take a page, skim it, toss it to the floor, pick up another page, and so on, his wire-rimmed glasses balanced upon the tip of his nose.

"Why's that?" he muttered absently.

Lorraine was stitching up a torn skirt, her sewing basket next to her on the couch. Although she could afford to buy new clothes, she was frugal, and sewing was one of her favorite past times.

Without taking her eyes off her sewing, Lorraine said, "Harlon likes you, so it seems."

"He *thinks* he does," said Eva. "But he's not my type. And I don't want him working for you anymore."

The last part she said to her father. His eyes moved up and down the paper, apparently trying to find his place. "Father! I don't like Harlon Hall and I want him fired!"

"I can't do that, Evalyn. He's exceptional at his job. He's already found us two new sites."

Eva blushed and her foot tapped the braided carpet. "He's a pest!"

Ian McClure laughed, that robust rumbling from his throat to his midsection and back up again. "Then stay away from him, sweetheart," he said. "Leave *him* alone."

This must be an inside joke, Eva thought when she realized her mother was laughing too. *They think I'm in love with him. They think I'm flattered by his attention!*

The next several days Eva absolutely tried to stay away from Harlon. If she spotted him in the distance, either at the mines or in Cambridge, she went the other direction. If she heard his name mentioned, she turned a deaf ear.

Two weeks later, there was a note from him left on her desk. She picked it up, squeezed it into a papery ball, and threw it into the trash can.

But she couldn't get rid of him. One afternoon in June, she went to Zanesville to meet a friend for lunch, and there he was. She managed to avoid him by walking in the opposite direction.

Thankfully, she didn't see him again until a warm September day when she drove out to the cemetery to put a bouquet of flowers on her great-aunt Meghan's—Lorraine's side of the family—grave.

After arranging the bouquet of white roses near the headstone and standing up to turn, she was startled by Harlon's voice.

"I'm so sorry, Eva," he said.

He had both hands in his trouser pockets. He was looking at the ground near his shoes. Hangdog was the thought that came to her mind—such despair, his expression seemingly genuine but infuriating.

"Harlon, you startled me. I want you to stop following me!"

"But I love you, Eva," he said.

There were two children with their mother near the road.

The children were chasing a butterfly. They seemed so carefree … happy to be alive.

"You don't love me, Harlon," she said sharply. "You don't even know me."

"I admire your stoic nature," he said. "You're an incredible woman."

Eva was clearly agitated. "I've never met anyone so vague!"

She was miserable in the early autumn heat, although she wore culottes to the knee and a flimsy cotton blouse with the sleeves rolled up.

There was a cement bench to the left of them near a row of maple trees. "Let's go sit in the shade," Harlon said. "Maybe have a chat."

"I don't have time to *chat*, Harlon. You should *know* that by now!"

But he wouldn't take no for an answer. He was already seated and patted the stone bench with his hand, indicating she should sit next to him.

"Sit, Eva," he ordered.

She walked over to him and sat down, leaving a few inches between them. He took a handkerchief from the pocket of his trousers and brought the cloth to his brow, dabbed his chin.

"Here's the deal," he said as they watched a butterfly hover above the forget-me-nots near the perimeter of the McClure family plot. "I want to marry you. I can be a big help to you in the future. My knowledge of minerals. The coal industry specifically. Not only that," he added with a forced voice due to the dry air. "I'm in love with you."

Eva laughed; a spontaneous rumbling similar to her father's.

He turned to look at the side of her face. She hoped he wasn't thinking that she looks more masculine than feminine.

All of her life, she was aware of her plain-Jane looks; however, she had been told there was a dainty tilt to her nose, despite its size, and her bustline, while not full, was adequate enough. Her last beau even said her blue eyes were "jewels from the earth itself."

Eva turned to look at him, her lips shaped into a smile. "You're insane, Harlon," she said. "But I'll marry you. On Christmas Eve."

• • •

There was an ice storm on Christmas Eve and Harlon was trapped at the McClure country home, surrounded by the scent of cinnamon and staring at a crackling fire in the stone fireplace.

Christmas music floated throughout the house. The reverend, a friend of the family, was detained due to the storm.

Lorraine seemed all aflutter but Eva was relieved, and as Harlon fidgeted, McClure apparently found the turn of events humorous. He grinned while holding an unlit cigar.

Nothing surprised him anymore. Nothing.

The decorations and food for the *Christmas Wedding*, as Lorraine had titled the event, cost six thousand dollars and counting. Thankfully, the caterers had delivered the dinner before the storm— salmon and butterfly shrimp. There were two dozen bottles of champagne delivered also, two cases of the finest bourbon, and one case of vodka.

The decorations were put up days ahead of time, throngs of draping pine ropes with entwined red velvet ribbons. Tall glass globes filled with poinsettias, at least fourteen of them, were put on end tables and bookcases, even the corner shelves. They were everywhere, these immense vases of poinsettias. So were the holly berry and ivy ropes, hanging from chandeliers, and mistletoe, of course, keeping the theme of a traditional Christmas combined with love.

The dining room was decorated in red, green, and silver for the dinner after the wedding ceremony. The long table had been moved to one end of the room next to the side hutch, and two tables of the same length were arranged at both ends. All three tables were covered with white satin tablecloths.

There was a seven-foot-tall Christmas tree decorated with red bows and white lights in a corner.

It was a rarity for a storm of such intensity to hit southern Ohio this time of the year. January or early

February, maybe. But on Christmas Eve? Lorraine found the oddity an unforgivable inconvenience, worse than any disruption she had ever experienced in her life.

For one thing, every year on Christmas Eve, Lorraine invited all the relatives from both sides of the family—the McClure's and the Robesons (her maiden name) from anywhere and everywhere throughout the region. They would stay at the local hotels, and some would even board at the McClure Homestead. There was never an issue with the weather until this year, the very year her daughter decided to get married. On Christmas Eve.

Of course, they had heard rumors on the radio of a cold front coming in from the north—warnings of ice mostly, and spurts of snow and viciously cold temperatures. But they didn't believe it.

Maybe this is a sign, thought Eva. *Maybe Harlon will see this as a reason to cancel the wedding.*

Harlon believed the opposite: he insisted the storm was saying, "You are meant for each other!"

"The wind has subsided," McClure announced, standing in the foyer of the dining room. He shoved his arms into a heavy gray coat. "I'm going to go get Reverend Timmons myself!"

"Oh, no you're not!" Lorraine said. "You're not going out in this dangerous weather to pick up Reverend Timmons who lives halfway to Marietta! The ceremony will be postponed! That's all there is to it! We'll have fun with this turn of events, you'll see; we'll eat the dinner this evening. The caterers have already delivered it and we'll simply have the ceremony tomorrow, on Christmas morning! Won't that be fun, dear?" She turned, her eyes darting in every direction. "Ian? Ian McClure! Where are-"

But Ian was already in his shiny black Lincoln and halfway down the driveway.

CHAPTER 15

The following morning after meeting with the realtor, Cassie was reading a newspaper on the screened-in back porch. She was drinking coffee and still wearing her pajamas. Mostly, the headlines were about the heat, but there was also an article entitled "Back in Time," featuring the big flood of June 1998. Cassie remembered it well. She remembered because the flooding caused problems for her family and neighbors, and for businesses on Route 209. There was devastation having to do with an overflowing of Wills Creek, located in the southern part of the city. *Interesting*, she thought. *So much to learn.*

Like the details of my grandfather's death.

Cassie wanted to know exactly what happened to him. Also, and foremost, she had heard a rumor from a friend who worked at the county clerk's office that Harlon Hall was murdered.

"Cassie!" yelled a familiar voice. It was Frances.

"I'm busy!" Cassie shouted back. "Whatever you want, it can wait!"

Cassie hated interruptions while reading the newspaper. She hated the very notion of Frances to begin with, which didn't help matters.

"That realtor Brian O'Dell called!" Frances screamed from the kitchen doorway. "I gave him your cell phone number! He's calling you back..." Apparently, Frances heard the ringing of Cassie's cell next to her on the wicker table. "Right now!" she said, still screeching.

"You shouldn't have given him my number! And his name's O'Dea!" Cassie watched her cell phone quiver. She grabbed it and pressed the answer button. "Yes?"

"Cassie? This is Brian O'Dea? With Sunshine Realty?"

She wasn't a fan of statements delivered as questions. To her, facts relayed as questions meant the person was insecure. Either he was or he wasn't Brian O'Dea with Sunshine Realty.

"Yes, this is Cassie," she said.

"Hi. I was wondering if we could meet today and walk through the Eighth Avenue house. I know I said I'd wait for your call, but two different couples are looking for a house just like yours in that location, and one family wants to move in before school starts this fall. They have children and —"

Cassie cut him off. "To tell you the truth, I might hold off on selling for now. I have so much to clear out of the house and garage, and frankly, I'm not in the mood for all the chaos."

"Yes, I understand that," Brian said, his sales pitch building, "but I'd love to walk through it with you. I'm curious about the house and the neighborhood. You see, my great-aunt used to live on the same street and it would be wonderful to look around. You know? Nostalgia?"

"Maybe," she said, toying with getting his ideas on the interior of her house. "But I'm very busy these days."

"It'll only be an hour of your time, tops," he said. He had switched from uncertain speech to confident. "It's a whim, I know. But it would be great to check it out."

Cassie rolled her eyes. She had planned on investigating the secret basement today when Grandmother and Frances left to go shopping. Once a month, the two would shop and have dinner out. "One hour," Cassie agreed, her voice firm. "I have a lot to do today. I'll meet you there at one o'clock."

"Fantastic!" he said. "I'll be there!" He hung up.

That's just great, she thought as she finished her coffee. *Right when I'm finally feeing relaxed. It must be a written rule somewhere that someone has to disrupt my solitude.*

She went back to the kitchen and put her china cup onto the counter. Someone was whispering. She stopped to listen, but she couldn't make out the words. There was a swooshing sound, gliding in the opposite direction.

She moved forward, following the sound. She stepped left, then right, towards the hallway. She stopped at the entrance, flat up against the wall. *Shhhhush . . . shhhooshh* was all she heard; then she realized there were two different pitches to the whispers, one higher than the other.

I . . . don't think . . . swoosh.

She moved closer to the hallway. She held her breath, trying to hear what the voices were saying. The pitch had risen, the two voices now arguing. She couldn't tell if Grandmother was involved in the conversation or not. And the other voice? Frances? One of the voices *had* to be Frances's. Who else would be in the house this early in the day?

She can't find out. Do you hear me?

Oh my God, thought Cassie. *They're talking about me.*

The realization made Cassie panic. She shouted, "Frances! What's for breakfast?" putting an end to the whispers.

Cassie felt sick to her stomach and angry with herself for not keeping quiet to decode more of the conversation.

"Oh, Frances?" she asked the balmy kitchen air in a sing-song manner. "Fran—nie?"

She heard the patter, slide, and slap of France's sneakers upon the wooden floor in the hallway, louder and louder until Frances entered the kitchen, both hands in fists, her mouth a grimace as if she had been taken from a life-altering task. "Surely you can pour cereal into a bowl," Frances sneered. "And top it off with milk that's located in the refrigerator. Which I'm sure you know!" Frances's face had turned so mean and ugly, Cassie wanted to smack her.

"You're paid to wait on *me*, Frances," Cassie snipped back at her. "You work here. I don't!"

"Is that right?" Frances asked, going straight for the coffee maker. She selected a cup and poured herself coffee, taking her sweet-old time. She also poured cream into the cup; and added a spoonful of sugar and stirred. "Let me tell *you* something, little girl. You have a house of your own. Live there, not here! Do *you* understand *me?*"

Cassie advanced toward Frances, almost up to the tips of her sneakers. "Oh, no way, Fran! *You* don't tell *me* what to do. I'll definitely stick around to look after Grandmother now! I know you're up to something! I hear you slinking around in the middle of the night! I hear you whispering and I *will* find out who you're sneaking in at all hours!" She wanted to slap the smirk off Frances's face. She wanted to yank her ratty hair right off her head.

"You little ingrate!" Frances seethed. She was so worked up, her teeth started to chatter. "I'm telling your grandmother how you mistreat me! I'm telling her I caught you and that boy—that Eric person—downstairs in the basement area that no one, and I mean *no one* is supposed to go into but her!"

"Oh! You just go right ahead and tell her, *Fran!* I'm pretty sure she'll want to hear all about how *someone* left one of the basement windows open! Naturally, Eric and I wondered why!"

Frances moved even closer to Cassie's face, so close Cassie could smell her body odor, disturbingly rancid.

Frances's breath was powerful as well, reminding Cassie of spoiled meat. "You listen to me, Cassie," she said. "If anything is missing from the basement, anything at all, *you* are to blame."

"Get away from me, Frances. Before I punch you in the nose!"

Frances backed up, apparently not wanting to find out if Cassie would follow through on her threat. Frances became mute. Her facial features and her posture turned statuesque. She backed away from Cassie and said, "I'll tell your grandmother you're waiting to have breakfast with her."

• • •

"Frances is agitated, Cassandra," said Eva when she pulled out a chair and sat down at the table across from her. "Do you know why?"

"No, Grandmother. I *did* ask her to make waffles, but apparently, she's too tired. Maybe that set her off. A simple request."

"Could be," Eva agreed. "I don't think she's feeling up to par lately."

Eva was wearing a pantsuit, different than the one she had on the other day. This time, she wore a pinkish-red shade with a white sleeveless shell beneath. A sheer texture, suitable for hot summer days. She wore pearl earrings and dark brown sandals. Her hair was twisted to the back of her head into a tidy bun. She looked like she was going to a business meeting.

Cassie finished her coffee. "You're dressed pretty smart for shopping, Grandmother," she said. "Today is your shopping-dinner date with Frances, yes?"

"That's right, we try to do this once a month." At the mention of her name, Eva turned in her chair. "Frances! Cassie wants waffles. Pretty sure you can manage that! We have plenty of time before we leave for the mall!"

"That's okay, Grandmother. I'm not hungry, and by the way, I'm meeting Brian O'Dea at my house at one o'clock. He talked me into a walkabout."

Eva clapped her hands. "That's wonderful news! You won't regret finding a brand-new home."

Cassie didn't want to commit to anything. Especially not until she figured out why there was a secret basement and why Frances was acting so protective of Eva. "We'll see."

"Good enough," Eva agreed.

Out of the blue, Frances appeared by Eva's elbow with the coffee pot and a pink cup. She put the cup down and poured coffee to the brim. She turned to the counter for the cream, and also the sugar bowl. "Just meet with Brian and see what suggestions he offers," said Eva. "That's all I ask."

Cassie saw Frances glare at her from the counter, but she turned away as soon as Cassie looked her in the eye. "I'm going to go upstairs and get ready," Cassie said. "You two ladies have a good shopping trip!"

"Very well," said Eva. "We'll be leaving in about a half hour. Please lock up when you go."

Cassie looked at Frances again. "Oh, definitely. I won't forget to lock *every* door and *window.*"

Cassie took her time walking down the hallway and up the stairs to the second floor. She listened, wanting to overhear bits of conversation but all she heard was small talk between her grandmother and Frances. "Let's start with Lindy's first, then over to the Shoe Shoppe." Then Frances's voice: "Good idea! I want to find a rug or two for my house as well. And maybe new bath towels, if we have time."

"We'll *make* the time!" said Eva, excitement in her voice. "And we'll have a nice quiet dinner at The Gold Lamb."

At the top of the steps, Cassie turned toward the direction of her bedroom. *This is ideal. I'll be here alone until I meet Brian at one. I'll finally get a chance to go back down to the basement and look around.*

Cassie went into the upstairs library, where she would get a perfect view of Grandmother and Frances backing Grandmother's BMW out of the garage for their shopping extravaganza. Cassie thought how nice that Grandmother has someone to go shopping and out to dinner with; although her choice of a companion, in Cassie's opinion, left a lot to be desired.

Cassie waited at the window. Sure enough, Grandmother and Frances walked over to the garage. Surprisingly, it was Grandmother who led the way, Grandmother who pushed the buttons of the electronic garage door, only to press again and again. Grandmother who went to the side door, disappeared inside the garage, and in a flash, hoisted the door up.

Cassie gasped. *What's this about?* How did she dismantle the electronics and lift the heavy door by herself?

Frances put a hand to her mouth, stifling a laugh. Then Frances turned and looked behind her, apparently making sure no one witnessed Eva's miraculous strength.

Frances waited at the white fence that separated the driveway from the backyard. Cassie noticed she had changed clothes as well. Her normal clothes were dowdy and frayed, but not today. Today Frances looked almost chic.

Frances had changed into a mauve skirt and matching short-sleeved jacket, and like Eva, she wore a sheer sleeveless top beneath the jacket. Her hair was shaped around her ears and her bangs hung down her forehead making her look younger—if one didn't look too long. There was a sparkling barrette holding part of her hair above her right ear.

She was wearing black flats on her long feet, and thanks to the dark color, her feet look smaller. An illusion, yes, but overall, her outfit provided a feminine touch.

Somehow, she looked attractive. Especially when she laughed. She looked like she was going on a real date, not with Grandmother Eva, thought Cassie, but with a man. Possibly the man of her dreams.

• • •

After Grandmother and Frances left the premises, Cassie dressed for her meeting with Brian O'Dea. That way, she could investigate the house and still have plenty of time to hurry out the back door to her car.

She wore a white short-sleeved blouse and denim shorts. She was happy to have lost weight. Happier still that the size eight shorts she bought two summers ago—that didn't fit last summer because they were too tight— fit perfectly now.

She put on sneakers, hoop earrings, and even mascara and a tad of blush. She worked her hair up into a ponytail. She grabbed her bag and car keys from the table next to her bed and pulled the door shut behind her.

She was so anxious to find the hidden stairway to the secluded section of the basement again, she almost tripped down the steps. That would have been a sight. She could have fallen all the way down the stairs and landed on the floor below with a broken neck.

Calm down, she told herself. *You have plenty of time.*

She had to picture the section of the house where she and Eric found the door to the steep steps and the narrow hallway several feet down where, she recalled, they discovered the basement door, dusty and cobwebbed.

She retraced the steps she had taken with Eric, and, as she walked to the back of the house, past the huge bay window in the living room and the second downstairs library, she decided Eric had lied to her. No way was he there only once with Grandmother and his father.

She went back to the stairway and to the library for a flashlight. She remembered there was a light switch halfway down the stairway to the basement, but worried that without a flashlight, she might not make it through the hallway in order to find the door.

She searched the library. In her frenzy to get on with her plan, she knocked a book off the second shelf by the left of the door. The book was a hardback and landed on the worn carpet with a loud bang.

She stared down at the book, spread open with an envelope sticking out of the pages. She bent over to pick up the envelope. Ten one-hundred-dollar bills were inside it. She thumbed through the book, finding another envelope, and opened it to another stash of five one-hundred-dollar bills. Realizing this might be the pattern of a person who felt the need to hide his or her money, she continued to go through more books. Fifteen minutes later, she had counted thirty-five one-hundred-dollar bills.

CHAPTER 16

Eva knew Harlon was worried about the wedding gifts that had arrived at the McClure's country estate when he asked her, "Do we have to return the gifts if the wedding is cancelled due to the storm?"

An ice storm on Christmas Eve, of all nights.

Eva turned her head away, and smiling, she lifted the glass of sherry to her lips. *Thank God for ice storms*, she thought.

"I'm not sure," she said. "I've never had my wedding ceremony interrupted before."

Harlon snapped his fingers as he paced up and down the hallway. At one point he turned, faced Eva, and laughed in a manic manner. "Oh damn!" he said. "I was hoping we could return all the gifts for cash!"

She lifted her glass in a toast. She was dressed for the ceremony: a long-sleeved, floor-length, off-white satin dress with lace around the neck and at the wrists and white slippers to match. Her hair was sculptured upward into an old-fashioned half-bouffant, a twisted wave at the back of her head threaded with pearls.

"Bravo to you!" she said, emptying the glass after two swallows. Then she turned and headed for the kitchen to see if she could snag a sandwich, a croissant, anything to ward off this woozy feeling.

• • •

After eating some mixed fruit and a roll, Eva joined Harlon on the couch by the fireplace in the drawing room. She handed him a glass of sherry. "Try not to worry, Harlon. Father will come through. He'll pick up the reverend and bring him here, directly. You'll see. Weather *won't* stop my father."

"I don't want you to be disappointed, Eva. You dreamed of a Christmas Eve wedding, and it's supposed to start in two hours. With this storm—"

"Shush!" said Eva. "There's plenty of time."

"I love this house," Harlon said wistfully. "It's so beautiful."

Eva was used to people complimenting her family home. Eva knew the whole story of her father coming alone to America from Ireland, working his way from New York to Ohio where he met her mother and married her before continuing onward to settle in Cambridge. Eva knew people said he had been charmed by finding 262 acres rich in coal. He built his business during a time period when unions were formed—a dangerous time of improving worker's rights and updates in equipment. A time when her parents lived in a one-room house; in fact, the very room Eva and Harlon were sitting in at present, staring into a warm, cozy fire.

Now, after many years of building up his mining business and adding on, the house truly was *grand* for lack of a better word. Two levels, tucked inside spruce and maple trees. The typical country mansion, painted white, with a front porch half the width of the house. The upstairs had five bedrooms, three bathrooms, and also a half-bath downstairs, off a den. There was also Father's study, the spacious kitchen, an elaborate dining room, a library, a cellar, and a basement. A large red barn was attached to the house by a hallway.

But Eva had already told her father that when and if she ever married, she wanted her own house built on the top of a hill on her own land. And Ian McClure had said, "Absolutely, my dear, but never, *ever* put anyone's name on the deed but yours."

"I could live in a house like this," Harlon murmured, his eyes closed as the fire and sherry made him drowsy.

Eva turned to study the side of his face. She noticed, for the first time, that his nose had an odd crimp to it; a bump so to speak, smack in the middle. He also had a loose chin, like a flabby pocket. He was beginning to bald at the hairline and graying at the temples. He had a pouch over his belt, or was she imagining this unsightly flaw?

She realized he was older than he had claimed. She realized, too, but couldn't prove, that Harlon Hall was a con man.

• • •

Lorraine ran out of the library, her pixie face flushed and her hands waving in the air. "Everybody! Ian just called. He has the reverend!"

"Hurry!" she yelled throughout the house. "Eva! Go freshen up! Your Christmas Eve wedding is going to happen!"

Eva had her eyes closed, dreaming about her new house. She wanted a Tudor-style mansion with rose gardens and two garages for her fleet of vehicles. She wanted at least 400 acres of land.

Next to her on the couch, Harlon twitched until his eyelids opened. The buzz of activity in the dining room down the hallway was startling, at least for Harlon, who by now had consumed too much sherry and rushed up to the decanter on the table by the window to pour himself a shot of vodka.

He couldn't stop shaking. He had been zapped to attention from his dozing, and so had Eva, who was still sitting on the couch, watching the fire in the fireplace. *I hope I'm dreaming all this,* she thought wearily.

"I told you my father would get the reverend," she said, realizing she wasn't dreaming at all; marrying Harlon was beginning to look like reality.

"Eva!" her mother shouted. "Come with us so we can put some final touches to your makeup!" With that remark Lorraine and her sister, Eva's Aunt Millie, barged into the study, pushed Harlon to the side, and whisked Eva away to the library behind the kitchen to "spruce" her up.

Eva was sluggish after only two glasses of sherry and hoped she wouldn't fall or trip during the walk down the hallway to the main living room where the nuptials would take place.

Suddenly, she was so weak in the knees her mother and Aunt Millie, along with Cousin Joan, had to help her through the kitchen. "And your father has a caravan of guests behind him," Lorraine explained. "All of them, Eva! Or at least most of them! The guests are still coming!" Lorraine passed Eva off to her sister and niece, as if she were a mannequin for them to dress up for display. "Take her!" Lorraine cried. "Do something with her. Her hair came loose from the pins! *Try* to make her pretty! I hope dinner isn't ruined!"

And off she went.

"I can't do this," Eva yelled at Aunt Millie, whose voluptuous cleavage, directly in Eva's face, smelled of sickening-sweet lilacs. Millie's dress was purple as well, and she wore a purple hat. All of her smelled and looked like lilacs—in the wintertime. "I can't! I'm not, *not* ready!"

"Oh, Evalyn," her aunt scolded. "After all this trouble, you most certainly *can!* And you *will!*"

Aunt Millie shoved Eva into a chair and started fussing with her hair, taking out pins, teasing clumped strands with a comb, and making sure the pearl clips were placed exactly as before.

Eva looked to Joan for help, but Joan was trying to pull Eva away from Millie, attempting to powder Eva's cheeks and nose. "Hold still!" Joan sneered. "The guests will be here any minute!"

"Quit pushing me around!" Eva shouted. "The guests can wait! Everyone can just wait!"

Eva looked at Joan, thinking that with Joan's overbite, flat chest, and unruly hair, she was a much better match for Harlon Hall.

Yes, Joan should marry Harlon. Not me!

Eva was so upset by this realization, she thought she was going to throw up all over her exquisite white dress. She steadied herself. *Why did I agree to marry Harlon?* She was doing fine on her own and turning into an old maid was the least of her worries. She could care less what people thought of her. All she wanted to do for the rest of her life was help her father with his company and manage his affairs after he was gone. Furthermore, she couldn't believe her father condoned this marriage. Why would he approve of someone like Harlon Hall? Her father never liked the men she dated. Although, she had only been out with three different men *ever* in her life, and the last man she almost married, but he vanished into thin air. Was her father worried she would die alone? Left all alone, after he and Mother passed away?

"Eva, my dear!" her father said to her from the library door. Her cousin and aunt were still fussing with her hair, but at the sound of Ian's voice, especially since she was just thinking about him, Eva jumped out of the chair and ran to him.

"You made it!" she said, trying not to cry.

"Yes! The reverend is here and so are most of your guests. Are you ready?"

She always told her father the truth. "No!"

He pulled her to him and hugged her. He whispered, "You don't have to marry him if you don't want to, Eva."

"I will," she said. "I like him well enough."

Ian laughed. The maid and a few relatives and friends who were within hearing range turned, startled by his robust laughter.

"I like him well enough!" Ian repeated, looking down at her with a sparkle in his eye. "Liking him is better than hating him, eh?"

"Father, I love you," Eva said, hugging him and not wanting to let go.

After the ceremony, the dinner dragged on far too long—four hours of feasting and drinking and loud Christmas music. Eva was so tired and disgusted, she wanted to die.

She would rather be dead than married to Harlon Hall.

CHAPTER 17

Cassie ran back to her bedroom upstairs to stash the money. She didn't want to take a chance that she might be intercepted. She needed to hide the money quickly before continuing to search the library and the basement.

Inside her bedroom, she looked for a hiding place, but nothing seemed secure enough. She started to panic. She decided that for now, she would stash the money at the bottom of a box of clothes that she still hadn't unpacked. This particular box was below another, to the right of the window.

She ran out of the bedroom and closed the door behind her. She had to get back to the library and search for clues as to who had stashed all the money and why. She had forty minutes left before she was to meet Brian O'Dea at her house on Eighth Avenue.

Frankly, he could wait. After all, he was the one anxious to get inside the house and look around, not her.

She retraced her steps back to the library. She studied the walls, the carpet, the cobwebs and dead insects. This particular library had been closed up for some time. Maybe years. True, Grandmother and her part-time maid, Frances, didn't need every room in the house at their disposal.

Keeping the entire house open would cost too much money: heating in the winter, cooling in the summer.

There were hundreds of books and dozens of framed pictures on the walls; some were etchings, others watercolors, mostly of fields and pastures. Several of them were watercolors of barns and fences, coves of pine trees, sunsets, sunrises, and so on.

A few of the pictures were crooked. Cassie wanted to straighten them, but she knew straightening would lead to dusting, polishing, and cleaning. She didn't have the time.

She pulled books off the shelves, checked inside them, and carefully replaced them. She looked for signatures. Most of the books had Lorraine McClure written on the first page, and dates, such as 1896 onward.

This had to be Great-Grandmother Lorraine's library, and the other room, near Cassie's bedroom, must have been Lorraine's study. Eva had explained to Cassie that after the remodeling, Grandmother Lorraine spent a lot of time in these two rooms. After Eva's father, Ian, died of a heart attack, Lorraine moved in with Harlon and Eva, but unfortunately, Cassie didn't remember her.

She was definitely getting to know her now via her books and the money she hid inside them.

The hidden cash told Cassie that Lorraine didn't trust anyone with her money; it also told her Lorraine was worried about *running out* of money.

Cassie opened a volume of Henry James's short stories and found a one-page love letter from a man named Jeremy.

My dearest, Lorraine: I think of you every day. I dream about you every night. I understand why you married McClure. I do. You wanted the security a man like

McClure can provide. I know that; however, I think you were mostly in awe of him. I curse the day he came to Ohio. I curse the day you met him at the pavilion. But I know you love him; and it was meant to be.

Fascinated as she was, Cassie didn't have time to read the entire letter. She folded the paper and slipped it inside her square bag, along with the money she had collected.

In her mind, Great-Grandmother Lorraine was reaching out to her, coaxing her to the library, not only to get to know her better through her passion for reading, but also to show her where money was stashed.

Cassie needed more time to explore the library and the hidden section of basement. She decided for now, she wouldn't tell Eric about the library, and she definitely wouldn't mention the money she had found.

She wished she hadn't agreed to meet Brian O'Dea at the house on Eighth. Who knew when she would be alone in Grandmother's house again? It was imperative she go back down to the basement and find out what else Grandmother Eva had tucked away in the cedar chest, what other clues she might discover about Grandmother's marriage to Grandfather Harlon and about his death. How much money did Grandmother have hidden in the cedar chest, along with her other treasures? Did she learn this method of stashing valuables from Great-Grandmother Lorraine?

Still, why would Grandmother Eva feel the need to hide jewelry and cash in her own house?

If only I hadn't agreed to meet Brian O'Dea.

• • •

Cassie was late meeting Brian. She wasn't sure she had locked all the doors to Grandmother's house, so halfway to Cambridge she turned around and drove back. She checked the side doors again, the back doors, and of course, the front door.

She was worried someone might break into the house while no one was there and it would be her fault.

She drove up the driveway to her house on Eighth and parked behind Brian O'Dea's gray Grand Am. He was sitting on the front porch steps, waiting for her. When he saw her car approach, he stood up and waved.

She stepped out of the vehicle into the familiar blast of heat. Once again, she longed for cool autumn air, even winter.

"Hi, Cassie," he said cheerfully. "I was about to think you forgot our meeting!"

"No. I had to run an errand. And besides, I'm only ten minutes late."

He seemed to be the type of person one meets for the first time and feels as if the friendship has gone on for years.

"Were you born here?" she asked. "You look familiar."

"No, ma'am!" He held the screen door open for her while she unlocked the front door. "My family moved here from Indiana when I was thirteen."

"But you look familiar," she reiterated, thinking how absurd to call her ma'am. "Did we go to high school together?"

"I'd say so. There's only one high school in town!" Again, quite cheerful. All smiles.

He followed her into the house. She noticed a moldy scent coming from the living room. The kitchen was off to the left of the living room, a small dining area to the right. There was a pantry by the refrigerator with cake and noodle boxes and cans of food still on the shelves.

"A spectacular kitchen," he said behind her. "I like the space and long counters and all the cupboards. All definitely perks."

"Hmmmm." She wasn't listening. She was thinking about the time Lee made a spaghetti dinner. He liked to cook; however, he wasn't good at it. He burned the garlic bread and the pasta was spongy.

"My husband did a lot of the cooking in this kitchen," she said in a shaky voice. "I miss him so much."

"Oh, I'm so sorry." Brian walked toward her, but stopped as if knowing it would be a mistake to touch her. He had a notebook, small enough to slip into his shirt pocket and he quickly tucked it away. He had already jotted down some notes, she noticed, but apparently, he decided there was nothing more to add, for now.

"I'm so sorry," he said again, this time in a stern voice. "May I ask how he died?"

"He had a heart attack," she said. "He was only twenty-eight."

Brian shifted his tall frame from leg to leg. "You wouldn't expect it from someone so young. That's just terrible."

She wasn't about to discuss Lee with a *realtor*, good-looking or not. He was a stranger to her and Lee wasn't any of his business.

But Brian continued asking questions. "Did he have a defective heart?"

She squeezed the shoulder strap of her purse until her fingers ached. "Yes, he had a hole in his heart, but they didn't know until the autopsy. Apparently, it didn't close properly at birth. Or so the coroner said. He was in his car, stuck in traffic in a rainstorm. He had a heart attack and crashed into the car in front of him."

Brian shook his head, stared down at the floor, and back into her eyes. "I'm *so* sorry," he said again.

She changed the subject by walking to the hallway near the stairs. "There are only two bedrooms upstairs and a bathroom," she said. "A big walk-in closet at the end of the hallway. Go up and look around. I'm going to get something I left in the living room desk."

He acted as if he didn't want to leave her alone. "Go see what you think of the upstairs," she said again, nodding toward the stairway.

"Will you be all right?"

"Of course. Go on upstairs."

She listened to his footsteps as he climbed the stairway. She hoped the bedroom wasn't a total mess. Probably not; she was good at keeping her house organized, as far as making the bed and cleaning the bathrooms.

Also, there was the extra room she and Lee used for storage and a makeshift office. It contained a sewing table and a desk with a computer and fax machine.

She heard Brian move from room to room. She could tell when he stopped at the storage room. She pictured him scrutinizing the clutter—her clothes not on hangers but flipped across the rack, her DVDs and CDs piled haphazardly on a shelf. There was also a table with mounds of different colors and textures of material.

She stood up and walked over to the desk by the front window. There were personal insurance and medical papers she needed to collect and take with her. She found the folders right away and sat down on the green tweed couch to look through the pages.

And wait for Brian.

CHAPTER 18

While Cassie waited, her thoughts shifted from missing Lee to finding the right person to buy her house. Brian seemed to be honest and hard-working as far as she could tell.

Grandmother is right. I need to move on.

But Lee had been important to her since the day they met in middle school.

Through the years they stayed in touch, met on weekends and during summer vacations. However, they went their separate ways after graduating from high school. He went to Ohio State University in Columbus and she to Ohio Wesleyan. After three years in college, she quit to go to Europe with two of her girlfriends. When she returned home, she wanted to go back to school and finish her bachelor's degree in business but thanks to her father's insistence, she took another year off to "think over her options."

Back then, her father gave her all the money she needed.

She had wonderful opportunities at her disposal, but when she returned to Cambridge, she met up with Lee Sullivan again. He was working at the insurance firm where she bought her car insurance.

She kept in contact with him by meeting for lunches and dinner dates. After several months, they decided it was time to move in together. They rented an apartment in Coshocton, and a few weeks later without telling either set of parents, they got married at the Cambridge Courthouse. When their lease was up at the apartment in Coshocton, they moved into the house on Eighth Avenue.

Cassie flashed back from her past with Lee to the present as she sat on the couch Lee himself had bought.

Thinking about him, sensing him moving around the rooms, believing that selling their house might mean giving him up entirely, Cassie started to cry and couldn't stop.

"You okay down there?" Brian yelled from upstairs.

Brian came back downstairs to find her on the couch, her face flushed from crying. He sat down beside her. "Everything will be okay," he said. "You'll be okay."

She dropped the envelope to the hardwood floor at her feet and covered her eyes with her hands.

He sat beside her, so patiently and still. "Take your time," he said.

A few minutes later, she was able to speak. "It's this house," she said. "Grandmother is right. I need to sell it and get on with my life."

"Could be." Brian's voice was so low, she wasn't sure she heard him right, although he was sitting beside her.

"What do you think of the upstairs?" she asked. "I hope it's not too cluttered."

"Not cluttered at all. The bedrooms are perfect for a small family; you know, a family just starting out. The upstairs hallway bathroom is the perfect size as well. I didn't go into the master bedroom. I heard you down here crying, so . . ."

She resented that she wanted to explain herself. "It's this house!"

Brian followed her when she stood up and climbed the stairway with a resurgence of energy. She went into the master bedroom, the bedroom she shared with Lee, and picked up clothing: a shirt draped across a rocking chair, her winter nightgown flung to the floor by the dresser.

She thought of the contrasts between her furniture and the furniture at Grandmother's. Grandmother's antiques were wooden and sturdy, Cassie's were cheap-veneer and plastic.

She chose a travel bag from the closet and filled it with hair accessories and makeup.

"See," she said with a sweep of her hand. "No bathroom. We used the one down the hallway. But as you know, there's a half-bath downstairs." He added the information to his notebook. "This house was supposed to be temporary," she said. "We were only going to live here for a year or two, then move out to the country. We wanted to buy land near my great-grandparents' house. Or buy the house itself. Have you seen it? It's so beautiful. My Grandmother Eva showed me pictures of it once. She grew up there and even married my grandfather there on Christmas Eve." Cassie's voice raced with excitement as she relayed the plans she had made with Lee. "Grandmother told me there was an ice storm that day and the ceremony was delayed. My great-grandfather went out in the storm to get the reverend and other guests." Cassie was speaking so fast; she dropped an item while filling the travel bag. "They *did* marry that night, on Christmas Eve, thanks to my Great-Grandfather McClure. She said the dinner party afterwards was grand! She says she has more pictures to show me. I need to see them and ask her all about it. It's so romantic! Don't you think?"

Brian nodded while he studied the windows.

"Lee and I agreed that one day, if possible, we would buy my great-grandparents' home," she continued, running out of breath. "It's two stories with a big attic and a front porch. The red barn is attached by an extension at the side of the house. Anyway, it's out on Route 40. The homestead where Great-Grandfather first discovered coal. You must have heard of him? Ian McClure?"

"Not really," Brian said, inspecting the ceiling for water damage.

He hasn't heard of Ian McClure? The coal mining baron of the 1920s thru 1960s?

"You sell real estate in this area and you don't know the history?" He stared at the seams of the ceiling and checked the walls. "I see," she said, turning back to pack.

"I know the history," Brian said suddenly. "I know about the old McClure farm on Route 40. The Richards bought it—Sandra and Brenden Richards. My parents know them. They're elderly. They will probably sell one day, soon."

Now he had her attention.

"I'm going to buy it!" she restated. "How much acreage do they own with the house? There used to be two hundred sixty acres or more, but after Great-Grandfather died, my great-grandmother moved in with my grandparents where Grandmother Eva lives now."

"Yes, the farmhouse you're talking about is on Cleary Road," he said, still scribbling on his notepad while studying the inside of the closet.

"You *do* know it?"

"Yes, I know it very well." He turned and caught her eye with his own. "Contrary to what you believe," he said, "I *do* my homework."

"How much land is still with the house?" Cassie asked. "Do you know?"

"Not exactly. But I'll find out for you."

"Good. Because I think Grandmother Eva and Harlon sold off parcels to a private developer. Probably thanks to that developer slash country club owner, what's-his-name. The man Grandmother hated so much. Harold something or other."

"Interesting," Brian muttered.

"I need to know what's left with the house. Hopefully, the barn's still there. I love the red barn!"

"I think they converted the barn into a garage," Brian said, now looking over the light-brown carpet. "With a skylight and a small porch, off to one side. But it's still red."

"That would be great if you'd check for me," Cassie said. "My Great-Grandmother Lorraine moved into the Everly house with my grandparents after Ian McClure died. Somehow, they—Eva and Harlon—got her to sign over the homestead." For the sake of conversational ease, she decided to drop the *grandfather* and *great-grandmother* and call them by their first names. "So, they sold it."

Cassie made a mental note to find out if they tricked Lorraine into signing the house over to them. Was that why she stashed money in her favorite books?

As soon as they were done inspecting the house, Cassie would go back to Eva's and search Lorraine's library again; maybe she could find out more about the homestead, and whether or not Great-Grandmother had been incapacitated, mentally or physically. Did she fall apart after Ian McClure had his fatal heart attack?

Cassie was completely motivated to sell her house on 8th Avenue. She would sell her house as is and put a down payment on the McClure Homestead.

Now more than ever, Cassie wanted to see the photos Eva mentioned she had of the house, the ones from years ago as Grandfather McClure built it in stages. And most importantly, she wanted to see Eva and Harlon's wedding photos.

"What do you think?" Cassie asked. "I'd like to sell as is, and quickly, if possible. I'm going to find out if the Homestead is on the market!"

"There are definitely strong possibilities here—" he started to say.

She was losing patience. "Can you be more precise? I can't put a lot of money into repairs; I'd rather take a loss on the sale price."

"If you want to sell as is, I don't see anything that raises a red flag." He rubbed his chin. "But I haven't been in the basement yet or in the garage and I need to find out how big the lot is. I need to get the house and property inspected and appraised."

"I'll be clearing the rest of my things out as soon as possible," Cassie assured him.

"Do you have papers regarding updates? The septic? The furnace? That sort of thing. I need to know how old they are and if and when any maintenance or replacement was done."

"Of course, I'll get right to it!"

She went back to the desk at the front window of the living room. "All the house papers should be in here.

This desk. It's where Lee kept papers pertaining to the house. I've been keeping up with the taxes and homeowner's insurance," she said proudly as she rifled through the drawers at the left side of the desk. "Here they are." She pulled out two thick folders and held them up for him to see but she wasn't going to hand them over until she reviewed the data herself.

Her life with Lee seemed like an eternity ago but instead of dwelling on his absence and falling into another emotional upheaval, she said, "I'll check through these and meet you tomorrow at your office."

Brian was quiet behind her. She turned, but he was still seated on the couch, looking down at his hands. "Are you…still with me?" she asked.

"I'm here," he said, but his jubilant personality had switched to a pensive one.

"I'll bring the folders to you tomorrow at your office," she repeated. "After I get a chance to go over them."

"You know," he said. "I've heard rumors."

"What do you mean?"

"About your grandmother. Like I said, they're probably just rumors."

Cassie didn't want to hear anymore. "I have to go," she said. "I'll call you in the morning and let you know what time I'll be at your office. Then we can go over these papers."

"Your grandfather's death was suspicious," said Brian. "You *do* know that, right?"

Cassie turned to look at him. First of all, her family history was none of his business, and secondly, maybe she should shop around for another realtor.

"I know my grandmother is still mourning his death," she lied. "And I know it's foolish to listen to gossip."

He stood up and rubbed his hands down the sides of his pants. "I shouldn't have said anything. People like to talk. I've also heard that her friend Frances has been implicated in criminal activity too."

They walked through the kitchen door at the side of the house, out to the driveway, and back into the scorching heat.

Cassie pretended she didn't hear him. She hoped she would get to the house before Grandmother and Frances returned. She wanted to investigate the basement and Great-Grandmother Lorraine's library further. It wasn't lost on her what Brian had said. *There is something sinister about Grandmother's past.*

And no one needed to tell her that Frances was not the *helper* and confidant she appeared to be.

CHAPTER 19

Frances and Grandmother weren't back yet but after parking her car in the garage and struggling to close the garage door with both hands, Cassie found Eric standing on the top step near the back porch of the house. He was tossing a key ring from hand to hand.

"Perfect timing," he said.

Cassie wasn't convinced Eric should have keys to every door of the house, but Eva had made it clear he was the only one she trusted. Just as she trusted his father before him.

Just as she trusted Frances.

"I hope you're here to fix the garage door," Cassie chastised, unsure about his intensions.

Something about Eric made her nervous; or, not necessarily nervous but on guard. He was a bit too arrogant to suit her, and having keys to every entrance of the house and all the outbuildings on the premises didn't improve her opinion of him.

"That's why I'm here," he said. "She called this morning and asked if I'd take a look at it. I have to contact the people who installed it though," he said, studying her over. "I can't fix it myself."

"What are you looking at, Eric? Please move aside so I can unlock the door."

He shoved his keys back into his pocket. "Is there a problem?" he asked. "You already know your gramma gave me a set of keys. I've always had them; I've always been here to help her. Where were *you?*"

Now he'd gone too far. "What do you know about it? About my family? About me?" she said.

Her heart was racing. "Move aside, please."

She opened the door and entered the back porch, now her favorite part of the house. Again, the cool, wide-open white room provided relief. "Were you going to go back down to the hidden basement? Tell me the truth."

"She asked me to go inside and check the AC," he said. "Something's wrong with the upstairs vents. Call her. Call her right now and ask her yourself."

"Never mind. I believe you. I was just at my house and I'm not feeling too well. I'll change clothes and be right back."

The first thing she did when she got to her bedroom was look inside the box of unpacked clothing where she had shoved the envelopes of one-hundred-dollar bills.

The envelopes were still there.

She knew she had to move her stash to a better hiding place. If only she had a safe or a strongbox, but she didn't. The best thing to do was deposit the money in her savings account first thing in the morning.

For now, she had to get back to Eric.

She changed into blue jeans and a white T-shirt.

She went back downstairs where he was waiting for her. "Let's go to the basement," he said. "I want to look around some more, and this is the perfect time. We're the only ones here."

"Fine. But we have to hurry. Grandmother and Frances could be back any time."

"We can always climb out one of the skinny windows if we have to," he said.

"You can, but I won't!"

He walked away and she followed. She felt out of place in the house without Grandmother present, but for some reason she couldn't explain, she liked being alone with Eric. She liked having his attention, feeling the surge of energy between them even though she felt guilty about being attracted to someone other than Lee.

When they came to the dark hallway, she latched onto the material of his shirt. No way was she going to suggest they get a flashlight from Lorraine's library . . . the library with all its treasures.

She held on to Eric's shirt as they descended halfway down the stairs, where he flipped on the light switch. "Have you been back here since Fran caught us?" he asked.

She thought it was humorous the way he called Frances "Fran."

"Why is it any of *your* business?" she asked.

He seemed refreshingly resilient against her stinging remarks. "Nice and cool down here," she said behind him. "Probably the coolest place in the whole house."

He didn't reply. He moved slowly, as if there were hidden cameras and they needed to dart from side to side in order to avoid them.

"I'm going straight for Grandmother's cedar chest," she said. "I want to see what other kinds of jewelry she has."

Cassie walked toward the stacks of wooden crates where she remembered finding the cedar chest. The *exact* same place. But it wasn't there.

"Eric! The cedar chest is gone!"

"It was Fran," he said. "She caught us down here so she moved it, or she had it moved."

"I knew I should have taken some of the money." Again, Cassie could tell by Eric's expression that he didn't approve of that idea. "Well, it's stupid of Grandmother to keep money down here anyway. In fact, I bet she forgot about it!"

Eric looked doubtful. "There's no way she could have forgotten about all that money, but I do agree, it's crazy to hide it down here."

Cassie pictured Frances taking the money, the jewels, the antique books. "Frances took it. That ugly old crow! She has no right to take my grandmother's things! I'm going to find out where and why! I'm going to confront her!"

"Then tell her what? That you came back down here *again* looking for the chest? If I were you, I wouldn't tip my hand."

"I can't let her get away with it, Eric! It's stealing! Who knows what else she's stolen? And over there"—Cassie pointed to the double-barrel twenty-gauge in the corner—"that's my grandmother's shotgun. She always keeps it in her bedroom. Grandmother and I noticed it was missing when I first moved in."

"Why would she have a shotgun in her bedroom?" Eric laughed at the very idea of it.

"Why do you think? She's afraid of something. Or someone!"

Eric diverted her focus from Frances to the large metal box he was looking into. "These clothes. Are they your gramma's?"

Cassie moved to the shadowed area where the metal box and at least a dozen cardboard boxes were lined up in a row. There were also old Christmas decorations, some antique, most of them cracked. She studied the clothes Eric held up—a cream-colored blouse and a pair of scuffed-up shoes. "Your gramma's?" he asked again.

"I don't know. She has a lot of blouses like this one." Cassie fingered the texture of the material, which was silky, but the color had faded and there was a dark stain and a rip near the shoulder area. Cassie shoved the blouse into her large bag. On second thought, she grabbed the shoes and stuffed them into her bag as well.

"This place makes me nervous," Eric said. He put the box back onto the wooden shelf where he had found it. "I don't even know why I looked in there. I guess I thought it might be an ammunition case. I was curious."

"I'm going to find out whose blouse this is," Cassie vowed. "And I'm going back upstairs to look for the cedar chest. It has to be around somewhere. Unless she walked out with the whole thing!"

Cassie pictured Frances waiting until Grandmother was asleep in her room. She could see Frances drag the cedar chest out one of the side doors of the house or maybe through the kitchen to the back porch. Drag it all the way to her car, load it herself, pull it up the cement steps and into her house in Cambridge. That shrewd, disgusting, ugly—

"I heard a car door shut," Eric yelled.

"You did not!"

"I heard a car door," he insisted. "Let's go!"

Cassie wanted to take the shotgun with her, but Eric was almost to the stairway and urged her onward with hand signals. "Hurry up!"

Halfway up the stairs, Eric snapped off the light. They made it to the landing and stopped to listen.

"No one's here," said Cassie. "Thanks for scaring me half to death."

"I heard something," he said. "I can't believe you didn't!"

She pushed him to the first step and down they went. Again, very slowly, and out the hidden door to the next floor—the second floor— where all the bedrooms were located. When Cassie was sure they were alone, she went to the library down the hall from Grandmother's bedroom and looked out the window. No one was in the yard and no one was near the garage.

She left the library, walked over to Grandmother's bedroom, and pushed the door open. Nothing out of the ordinary. For a second, she thought about going in and looking around but she couldn't bring herself to invade Grandmother's privacy. She wanted to believe that there was an unspoken bond of trust between them.

Cassie moved on down the hallway and found Eric standing in the doorway of her bedroom. "So, how's the air in here?" he asked. "The vents working all right? The lighting?"

"Yes, everything seems to be fine," she said.

Eric walked into her bedroom to check the windows.

"Are you comfortable staying here?" he asked.

"Yes. There's plenty of room."

"Kind of *too* big," he said, hands inside his pockets as he strolled around her room. "Kind of spooky," he added, looking down at her.

"There's plenty of room and—"

He came closer. "I shut the shop early today. Your gramma asked me to check the air-conditioning and the garage door. Oh, I already told you that."

"Yes, you did. Was it the vents? Did Frances close them off or something?"

"No, the vents are all open." He put two fingers against the side of her face. "I'm going to kiss you. I hope that's okay."

CHAPTER 20

Ian McClure had a luxurious three-story Tudor-style house built for Eva and Harlon, just as he had promised. When she was a teenager, he told her that if and when she married and wanted to start a family, he would give her the gift of her own home. On her own land.

But again, he advised, "Never put his name, or anyone else's, on the deed."

"Don't worry about that, Father," she said while going over the blueprints with him for the screened-in porch and two garages.

The rest of the house was already finished—that is, the main structure with three levels and long stairways and hallways.

Eva was delirious with happiness. She loved the house more with each passing day. She felt like she was drifting through a dream . . . drifting though her very own *dream* house.

Ian even let her assist with the designs. He paid for the project, of course, but she insisted on helping him pay for some of the furnishings and also the wallpapering in the bedrooms, carpeting, lighting fixtures, and so on.

She wanted to help build her own house.

Harlon, on the other hand, was away on business during most of the construction.

He told Eva he couldn't stand the pounding of nails, the banging of equipment, the noise at all hours.

Which suited her fine. In fact, she had agreed to marry him knowing he wouldn't be around much. He was restless. He liked to travel. She knew this from the beginning, and frankly, these traits made him the perfect husband for her.

Yes, she wanted her own house and possibly one child, but she had never, *ever* wanted a husband.

Not only did Harlon travel for his surveying job, he also took extra courses via the community college in Zanesville and the university in New Concord. He was always trying to improve his skills.

In fact, beginning in the nineteen sixties, as her father warned, the demand for coal as the primary fuel was expanding to natural gas. There were rules, more stipulations. The Environmental Protection Agency, the United Mine Workers Union, these organizations were always adding new criteria for miner's rights and updates for safer equipment.

Harlon had to stay ahead of the game. Eva understood and respected his willingness to keep in step with the changes, year after year.

Ian McClure, however, had semiretired and hired an assistant. The assistant was checking into more under-ground mining possibilities. Harlon, as McClure's son-in-law, would remain the top geologist working for McClure Mining.

Eva noticed Ian was aging rapidly—not surprising for a heavyset man who loved to eat, drink, and above all, be merry.

Lorraine once told Eva that she had always suspected Ian had a mistress or two. Lorraine said her husband had peculiar urges and he sometimes wanted to do *things* she preferred *not* to do.

"He was and always will be a carefree, spontaneous man," she lamented. "A lover of women."

That way, he left *her* alone, unless she wanted to be touched. If she didn't, Ian was willing to take his sexual peculiarities elsewhere. "Such an understanding man," Lorraine would say. "Such a dear, dear, sweet man."

She confided to Eva that she would always love Ian no matter what he did. Only one man came close to inspiring the feelings she had for Ian. His name was Jeremy. "A childhood friend," Lorraine confided, "who still writes love letters to me. I have nothing to hide, and neither does Ian."

Eva was accustomed to the open-minded, eccentric attitudes of her family members. To Eva, it was a given: the men wander and the women don't care.

Eva knew that her mother kept very active, in her own way. Lorraine collected first edition books and spent hours in her private library at the country homestead. She also enjoying sewing and designing patterns for handmade quilts, tablecloths, curtains, and even women's clothing.

Since Eva married Harlon, however, Lorraine spent a lot of time at the Tudor House on Everly Road, helping decorate, clean, organize, and plan.

"This house is spectacular!" Lorraine told Eva more than once. "You're such a lucky girl! My father couldn't wait to get rid of me! And *you!* You, my dear daughter, have a father who will stop at nothing to give you your heart's desire! Of course," she said with a finger to her forehead, pretending to revisit her childhood, "my father was a pauper.

Your father happens to be *very* rich! A self-made rich man!" she emphasized self-made and laughed.

She was about to take another sip of wine but Eva took the crystal glass from her bejeweled hand and said, "Mother, you've had enough."

But Lorraine's visible happiness was contagious.

And Eva couldn't think of anyone else she would rather help decorate her new house than her mother.

• • •

Harlon's absence was even more exhilarating than Lorraine's creative instincts. He annoyed Eva in so many ways.

His profile—that oddly shaped head, bald and melon-shaped, much too round for a human skull and dotted with scabs and bug bites. He was often scratching himself. Eva wondered if he had allergies, possibly to the country lifestyle. Or to women.

His nose—too large and ridged, often flaking off in public. And not from him picking it, which he did, unconsciously or knowingly.

His teeth were borderline yellow. He drank too much coffee and she suspected he smoked on the job. Never around her, mind you, but she could smell cigarette smoke residue on his clothes.

Which made his breath stink to high hell. She couldn't stand to kiss him. She couldn't even stand the *thought* of kissing him. His breath and his wet, wiggly lips made her gag.

He was always lying to her:

"Darling," he might say. "I have a geologist conference next week in Florida, in the Miami area. I'll be gone all day, every day. You wouldn't like it."

To agitate him, she'd respond, "Florida? I have friends in Miami, Harlon. I could call them up and go shopping with them while you are in your meetings. Perfect!"

Out of the corner of her eye, she watched him fidget. "But you'd be bored out of your mind the rest of the time, Evie," he'd say.

Or he might inform her at the drop of a hat, "Eva, darling, I have to go out of town for the night. Spur of the moment. I'll just pack a bag and leave you to your house activities. No problem!"

She'd cry out, "Nothing's as important as you, Harlon! The house can wait. I'd be happy to go with you. Where to?"

He would blink at the question of where to. "Oh, just …" She could tell he was trying to think up a humdrum location. "Just to Marietta. I have to look over a possible mining site."

"Harlon, I love Marietta. Give me time to pack a bag!" She'd even clap with false excitement.

"You wouldn't enjoy it," he'd say, perspiring. "It's just one night. I'll be back before you know it."

She finished the charade with a pout. "Fine. I'll go with you another time."

She whisked out of the room smiling, leaving him to pack.

• • •

Two weeks after the house and grounds had been completed, right before Thanksgiving, Eva pushed Lorraine into her bedroom and closed the door behind them.

"Mother," she said, wringing her hands. "I'm pregnant."

Lorraine covered her mouth. "Oh dear," she said through her fingers. "That's quite the feat, with Harlon gone so much of the time."

"Mother! The baby's Harlon's. Why would I have a lover?"

"I don't know *why*, dear. It's just that Harlon seems to be out of town a lot. And not too long ago, I saw a man leave your bedroom—"

"You were seeing things. I never—"

"Whatever you say, Eva. I understand how a woman can get lonely, trust me."

"What if the child looks like Harlon, Mother?"

Lorraine rolled her eyes and laughed. "You'd better hope it looks like him, Evalyn." She busied herself by straightening the heavy brown-and-white checked comforter on the king-sized bed.

"Oh God!" Eva screamed, bending over and holding herself. "He's so ugly! That big nose! The bowed legs! I can't stand it! I can't stand *him*! What will I do if it's a boy and looks like him? What"—she was now hysterical— "will I do if it's a girl, Mother? A girl … and she looks like … *him!*"

Eva collapsed onto the bed, knocking Lorraine to the floor.

CHAPTER 21

Cassie was so stunned by Eric's love-making techniques, she almost fell off the bed. She was even more shaken by her willingness to let a man other than Lee touch her, explore her, take her all in.

She was partially naked, in a flimsy shirt and bra, and he was still wearing his pants, although they were down around his knees.

She thought she heard a door slam downstairs, and that's when she jumped and almost fell to the floor. Good thing Eric was holding her.

"They're back!" she said.

But she didn't want to let go of him.

Eric moved his lips down her neck. "Who cares?"

She slid out of bed, put her jeans back on, and stepped into her shoes. "You've got to go. You've got to get out of here!"

He laughed at her. He got off the bed and pulled up his pants.

"I'll just go out the secret passage," he said, smiling. "The back way," he emphasized. "You know? The secret—"

"Dammit, hurry!" Cassie opened the door to listen for voices. She put a finger to her lips, but the more she warned him to be quiet, the more he made fun of her.

He was fully dressed again and followed her to the hallway. They walked to the door that led to the stairway and out of the house. She pushed him until he disappeared, all the way.

"Grandmother! Are you back?"

"Yes, Cassandra!" Grandmother yelled from the kitchen. "Come see what we bought!"

Cassie made it to the kitchen in time to see Frances put the bags onto the table. Frances was smiling. Her face was glowing from the sun, or maybe she only looked healthier because she had been out and about on a shopping spree.

"We hit two sales," Frances said. "And I found curtains for my bedroom. Towels and mats for my bathroom!"

Eva, however, was sitting at the table, seemingly catching her breath. "Oh, Cassandra," she said, her voice higher than normal. "You really should come with us next time. We have such fun! Don't we, Frances?"

"Absolutely!" Frances was making fresh coffee. "We bought two pies. We bought cherry and a vanilla cream!"

"That's nice, but I'll pass," said Cassie. She had *never* seen Frances this happy before.

"Suit yourself," said Frances. She was dividing up both pies; apparently, she and Grandmother were going to sample both.

Cassie sat down next to Eva, inspecting her face. "You aren't stoned are you, Grandmother?"

Eva and Frances laughed. They laughed so hard they couldn't speak. "Grandmother!" Cassie demanded.

"You're so funny, Cassandra," said Eva. "Of course not! We're just happy. Anything wrong with being happy?"

"Hmm!" said Cassie. She pushed herself away from the table and walked out onto the porch, her favorite place to read.

Grandmother and Frances were chattering and laughing in the kitchen behind her. Cassie looked for the current newspaper but each one was dated the previous week. And, she realized in her haste to dress and get rid of Eric, she had left her cell phone upstairs on the dresser.

She was thinking maybe she would sample the pies, after all.

She stood up and walked toward the kitchen, but suddenly, she stopped. Grandmother and Frances were kissing each other on the lips, tongues moving in and out of their mouths.

• • •

Cassie cleared her throat before entering the kitchen. "Grandmother," she said, pretending to read the paper held at arm's length in front of her. "I have a quick errand to run. But I need to go get my cell and my keys. Anything you need from the store while I'm out?"

Eva straightened up at the table. "No, dear. We're fine. Why are you going out this time of night? For what errand, exactly?"

Cassie tried not to look at either one of them. "It's only eight o'clock. I just need to run a quick errand. I'll be back before you know it."

She rushed through the kitchen, down the hallway and up the stairs toward her bedroom. Her head was spinning. She wanted to dive onto the bed and hide. *Grandmother and Frances*, she thought. *I can't believe it!*

I'm going to be sick.

Pull yourself together, she told herself. *Change clothes and go for a drive. Go to the Eighth Avenue house. See what else needs to be done.*

She still had cleaning supplies at the house and maybe now would be a good time to clean, work through her frustrations. She would toss away unnecessary items, maybe scour the kitchen floor, bleach the sink.

She knew she had to sell the house in order to have a down payment to buy the McClure Homestead.

She would contact Brian O'Dea later today, or first thing in the morning, and make it clear to him she was ready to start the marketing process.

Brian said he would contact the owners of the McClure Homestead to find out if they were thinking about selling. He would also find out how much acreage was left with the house.

She changed into a short-sleeved blouse and grabbed her phone and handbag.

She was relieved that Grandmother and Frances weren't in the kitchen when she came back downstairs. She heard the television on somewhere in the back of the house and peeked into the living room area where she found Grandmother on a recliner, Frances sitting on the couch with her feet propped up.

How cozy you two lovebirds look, Cassie thought bitterly.

They were still wearing fancy shopping clothes and they were focused on the television screen, but Cassie couldn't tell what they were watching. Thankfully, they weren't stuck together on the couch.

Cassie shuddered and ran back through the kitchen to the porch, locking the door behind her.

135

She drove along the trek of the winding driveway down Everly Road, turned onto another winding section of road, and finally onto Highway 40 toward Cambridge.

She turned the radio on full blast. Classical music. Violins and harps. She let her mind drift away from the vision of her grandmother kissing *the help*. Kissing Frances. Cassie concluded: you think you know someone so well, all of your life, and find out later what you *thought* you knew was the opposite of the truth.

No one is who or what they seem to be.

Cassie drove into the driveway at the Eighth Avenue house and sat there for several minutes, maybe longer. She had to relax and think. Come up with a plan.

She got out of the car and walked up the cement steps to the side door off the kitchen. She was able to see, thanks to the dusk-to-dawn lights.

Evening had fallen, yet the air was still sticky and humid.

For the first time in two years, walking up these steps and through the kitchen door didn't make her think of Lee. Lee would always be her first and only true love.

But for now, he had to step aside.

The house was comforting to her, almost a relief to be here this time, focused on cleaning and organizing. Away from everyone. She decided she would take only what things she needed, and leave the rest behind.

She spent two hours going through the kitchen cupboards. She put donated items—certain pots and pans and miscellaneous utensils, hand towels, and so on—in one box and the items she wanted to keep and use later in another box. She tossed garbage, such as outdated coupons and string, twist ties, old sticky notes, frayed rubber bands, in the garbage can.

At least it was a start.

She knew the task of dividing necessities from useless sentimental junk wasn't going to be easy. With *necessities* in mind, she skipped the living room and headed upstairs. The living room held nothing she wanted; in fact, she and Lee hardly ever spent time in there. They were either working or on the go.

She didn't even remember watching television together, although they probably did during the holidays. She flashed back to Christmas. She could see a tall decorated tree in the front window of the living room. So stunning, so incredibly beautiful with ornaments old and new; most of them she had purchased with Lee. The pine-scented candles, the music, the warm air radiating from the heaters.

Every Christmas Eve they would promise each other that by the next Christmas they would have a baby or expecting one.

It never happened.

Thankfully, however, this time, when her thoughts found Lee, she would not stay there. No more dwelling on what could have been.

The "if only he had lived."

For now, her goals were clear: sell this house, save her money, and buy the McClure Homestead.

• • •

The next morning Cassie called Brian O'Dea. "I need to know how much acreage is with the McClure Homestead," she explained again. She was sitting at the kitchen table with coffee and a pad of paper for her notes.

She could hear someone walk up behind her but the person in question must have overheard part of her conversation with Brian because the footsteps stopped.

"Yes," she said into her cell. "I see." She glanced behind her. "One minute, Brian." She turned to find Eva standing in the doorway next to the refrigerator, obviously trying to eavesdrop. "Hello, Grandmother. Sit down and have coffee with me. I'm talking with Brian about the Eighth Avenue house."

Eva was dressed in her gardening ensemble: blue linen pants, short-sleeved blue-and-white checked blouse. Her garden shoes and her big floppy hat were on the back porch where she would grab them when she was ready to go outside.

Eva smiled, reluctantly. "Hello, dear."

Cassie could tell Eva was apprehensive. Apparently, she had been alerted to the fact that Cassie saw something she shouldn't have.

Eva poured herself a cup of coffee, added a splash of vanilla creamer, and sat down at the table across from Cassie. She sipped and stared at Cassie and then lifted her gaze over Cassie's shoulder. As if in a trance.

Cassie said into her cell, "Very good, Brian. I'll talk to you later," and tapped the end call button on her cell.

Eva said, "That's wonderful. You decided to sell?"

"Yes," said Cassie. "I think it's time."

"Good for you, Cassandra. Grief can stunt your growth. Trust me, I know." As she spoke, her eyes never left Cassie's. She sipped from her cup, and lowered the cup to the saucer.

"Grandmother, I want to know what happened to Grandfather Harlon. You said he died in a car wreck?"

"No, dear. He had a heart attack, like my father. Very tragic. He was away on business and fell over dead. In a restaurant. Right in front of his lover."

Cassie stared at her napkin. "He was having dinner with his mistress?"

"Something like that, yes."

"It's—" She wasn't sure what to say. Eva seemed so accepting, so calm about her deceased husband's indiscretions. "It's very sad. I'm sorry, Grandmother. I don't remember his funeral, and we didn't get to view his body. My dad said even *he* didn't get to say goodbye."

Eva shrugged. She leaned against the table on her elbows and took another sip of coffee. "He looked so unlike himself, I thought it best to have him cremated immediately. It was such a shock, Cassandra, I couldn't bear to drag it out with a memorial service. We had a wake, in his memory, and I buried the urn myself."

"You told me before that a man named Harold Larrabee was at the same hotel in Columbus when Grandfather died. But you also said they were business partners." Cassie sensed a shift in Eva's mood—at the mention of Harold Larrabee.

"Yes, Harold was there," she confirmed. "They went on business trips together."

"Larrabee was a wealthy land developer, I think you said?"

Eva sat up straighter in her chair. "What exactly do you want to know, Cassandra?" she asked, her eyes hard on her granddaughter.

"Was Grandfather Harlon murdered? I need to know."

Eva shook her head and closed her eyes.

CHAPTER 22

Eva's son, Roy, was born in her bed at the Tudor House on Everly Road. The birth happened three weeks prior to her due date on July 18 at 9:35 in the morning. There was a midwife and a doctor present.

Of course, it was a blistering-hot morning, humidity clamping her to the soaked mattress despite the air conditioner and fans spinning from all directions.

As she lay screaming in pain.

Giving birth to Roy.

Eva had help after the birth. Not only did Lorraine live with them for a while, but Harlon hired a nurse to stay with Eva around the clock and help with the baby. Therefore, the nurse had to sleep in a guestroom— with the baby—get up with him every couple of hours, eventually taking turns with Lorraine.

The baby didn't sleep through the night until four months later.

Eva vowed she would *never* get pregnant again and she would *not* rely on birth control or condoms.

Two months later, when Harlon was away on one of his business trips, Eva scheduled a hysterectomy. It was well worth the pain, not to mention the two-week recovery. She didn't tell anyone about "the procedure," not even Lorraine.

Thankfully, Roy wasn't ugly as she had predicted. No blonde Adonis, certainly, but instead of good looks, Roy was endowed with intelligence and perseverance. He earned As and Bs all through grade school and high school. He graduated from college with high honors and two degrees.

The week after he graduated, he interned with a prestigious accounting firm in Dayton. After two years, he received an offer to work as an electrical engineer in Columbus, and the company also paid for extra courses. A course per month, along with his job, improved his skills and increased his paycheck.

While living in Columbus, he met Rachel. She was working as an LPN at Riverside Hospital, hoping to go back to school part-time and become an RN, but she married Roy instead. Only one year later Cassie was born.

Because Roy traveled often for his job and also taught courses at Muskingum University in New Concord, fifteen minutes from Cambridge, he moved his family closer to the university.

And closer to his parents, Eva and Harlon.

Roy soon noticed that his parents didn't spend much time together. They rarely attended family functions; not even holidays or birthdays. These facts prompted Roy to worry about the estate.

If his parents split up, no telling what might happen to his inheritance.

Days after Cassie was born, Ian McClure had a fatal heart attack and Eva and Harlon shocked Roy by selling the McClure Homestead, along with hundreds of acres of property elsewhere and half of the mining shares.

Roy thought he would never recover from this *god-awful surprise.*

In fact, from that day on, Roy's health started to decline. Furthermore, his grandmother, Lorraine, moved in to the Tudor mansion on Everly Road.

Roy noticed right away that Eva catered to Lorraine. With some of the money from the homestead sale, she renovated sections of the mansion to accommodate Lorraine's needs. Lorraine ended up with an entire wing of the house to herself: a private bedroom and bath, a sitting room, a library, and a room just for her clothes and accessories.

Roy knew Eva adored her mother, but in his opinion, investing thousands of dollars in her needs and whimsies was sheer nonsense.

All of her life, Lorraine McClure maintained a fit and trim figure, but unfortunately, her mind turned feeble. She stared out the window for hours at a time and lapsed into conversations with Ian. A flirtatious dialogue: "You're so handsome, Ian. The best-looking man and lover I've ever known!" Or she would say out loud at the drop of a hat, "I love you, Ian! Don't forget me!"

Right in the middle of Roy's success, Harlon was pronounced dead at a popular restaurant in Columbus, Ohio.

The news of Harlon's death, which came from a mysterious anonymous caller, was so unexpected the entire family went into hysterics, particularly when they couldn't find Eva.

Eva had left the day before Harlon to visit friends in Delaware, north of Columbus. What upset Roy the most was that Harlon claimed he was going to Cleveland to look over some properties when in fact, he was found dead in Columbus.

Roy called Eva's friend, Mallory Hinton, hoping to locate Eva before she heard of Harlon's death from a stranger, or perhaps the local news, but Mallory said Eva came by for lunch two days prior, and directly after, she went on her way. Eva didn't mention where she was going, reported Mallory, and as was Eva's custom, she rented a vehicle for the trip.

At least by renting a car Roy knew he could track her down if need be.

Roy rushed home from Atlanta where he was researching an extension for an apartment complex. He was about to assess its electrical capabilities when he got the disturbing call about his father. He asked the caller who he/she was but after relaying the news, the caller hung up. He couldn't tell if the voice was a man's or a woman's disguised as a man's. Certainly, Roy would need to get to the hotel in Columbus and fill in the gaps.

He told Rachel to pack their suitcases. His plan was to take Rachel and Cassie to the Tudor House before he drove onward to Columbus. No doubt a family member would need to identify Harlon Hall's body and if they couldn't locate Eva, Roy would be the one.

Frances was on vacation, which meant there was no one to help Rachel manage the house except for a substitute cleaning woman, who came in once a week.

Roy left Rachel and Cassie alone at the mansion and told Rachel before he left, "The second you hear from my mother, let me know!"

CHAPTER 23

"I'm not sure," Eva admitted to Cassie's question of Harlon's death eight years ago. "I don't know exactly what happened to him. But I suspect Harold Larrabee had something to do with it. Larrabee was a devious man. He could talk Harlon into anything. Harlon was always wanting money for Harold's investments."

"He asked you for money?" Cassie asked. "For the investments?"

"Yes, all the time. And he asked other people too. Maybe he owed the wrong people money and the stress was too much for him."

Cassie had always suspected that Grandfather Harlon had gotten in over his head with money issues. "Did he have heart problems? You told me the death certificate said the cause of death was a heart attack."

"True, it was a heart attack, but I've always wondered if someone caused it. I mean, other than his mistress, who was young enough to be his daughter." Eva's voice amplified the more she talked. "And he sure wasn't that athletic!"

Cassie touched Eva's arm, hoping to get back to the point of Grandfather Harlon's life. "Can I see your wedding pictures? I remember you showed me pictures of the

Homestead once and the mines, and you said you also had photos of your wedding day. I'd love to see them."

Eva shook her head. "I'm not sure where they are."

"Could I see Grandfather's military records too?"

Eva gave her a suspicious look. "*Why*, for goodness sake?"

"Family history. I want to know about my ancestors."

Eva stood up. "I don't know where his papers are. He wasn't in combat or anything of that nature. He wasn't a war hero, by any means. He learned about geology and finished school after the war."

"Still, I would like to see his military records, Grandmother. I'd like to see any pictures you have."

"I'll go to my study and look." Eva shuffled off towards the next section of the house. "You stay here!"

"I'm coming with you!"

Cassie followed, whether Eva liked it or not.

• • •

Cassie couldn't believe the changes to Eva's bedroom. Eva had actually tried to shut Cassie out by pushing the bedroom door against her. "What are you doing!" Cassie said, pushing inward as Eva pushed outward. "What do you have going on in here?"

Eva gasped when she realized Cassie was stronger than herself and there was no choice but to let Cassie enter.

"Where's your bed?" Cassie asked.

"Folded up and packed away. I told you. I'm making some changes around here."

"Where do you sleep?"

Eva headed toward a door near the closet. "I've been sleeping in the library. Come with me."

The room Eva had previously used as a study was completely different; the dingy floral wallpaper was gone and the walls had been painted brown and green. The antique furniture had been replaced with a modern overstuffed brown couch and matching recliner. In one area, there was a brass-framed, king-sized canopy bed. Near the bed was a wooden desk with a black swivel chair. There was a door by a corner and Cassie assumed this door was an entrance to a walk-in closet.

"You've been busy," said Cassie. "This is beautiful!"

Eva waved away Cassie's praise. "I've looked everywhere for the collection of pictures. Pictures of my childhood, my parents' home, the mining town, and even my wedding album. I can't find them. I think they've been stolen." Eva sat down in the plush recliner, shoved a lever to the floor with her right hand, and up went her feet. "I'd sure like to know who stole my pictures!"

Cassie suspected that Eva was putting on an act. "Where have you looked? I'll help you."

"I've looked everywhere. I just told you that!"

Cassie opened the top drawer of Eva's desk, whereby Eva shook a fist and hissed, "Tut-tut! Out of my personal things!"

"Exactly what did Frances tell you, Grandmother?"

"Nothing. I simply demand my privacy!"

Cassie went over to Eva's recliner, that oddly resembled a throne. She sat down on the edge by Eva's long, slippered feet. "Why can't I know things?" Cassie asked. "You said you want to give me your home one day. That must mean you trust me with it. I want to help you organize. I want to preserve our family legacy."

She knew she got Eva's attention with the "family legacy" bull. Part of this Cassie had meant. She truly did cherish the homestead Great-Grandfather McClure had built and she was planning on buying it.

"Tell me, Grandmother. What's up with you and Frances? What really happened to my grandfather?"

Eva straightened herself in the recliner and lifted her chin in that arrogant, know-it-all way of hers. "You read too much into every day, monotonous activities. My life is *not* as mysterious and dramatic as you think."

But Cassie could be just as arrogant. "You and Frances have something going, Grandmother. I saw you!"

"Are you suggesting I swing both ways, Cassandra?" Eva's upper lip twitched. Her left eyelid fluttered.

Cassie sighed. "I could care less what you two do. I only want to see some family pictures!"

"Then go downstairs to the gallery in the sitting room," Eva stammered. "And leave me alone. I'm taking a nap before dinner. Now scat!"

"Fine!" Cassie was satisfied by the fact that she had taken a key ring out of the desk drawer when Grandmother wasn't looking. One of the three keys had to be to the door near the far-left corner.

• • •

Grandmother knows fully well there are no wedding photos in the family gallery downstairs, thought Cassie. *When she's in the kitchen or watching television in the living room, I will sneak back to her new bedroom and get inside that other room. I have to find pictures of her wedding to Grandfather Harlon.*

Cassie also wanted to find Grandfather's military papers again. She should have grabbed them when she found them the first time among other items inside the cedar chest. She knew from her father that Harlon had joined the army during the Korean War and he obtained his degree via the GI Bill.

Cassie was halfway down the stairway when her cell rang. It was Brian O'Dea. She pressed the accept button. "Yes?"

"Hello, Cassie," said Brian. "I've been doing some research for you, as you requested. Sandra and Brenden Richards bought the homestead house on Cleary Road twenty-three years ago from your Great-Grandmother Lorraine Robeson McClure. I checked with the county clerk's office and also a plat book. Anyway, the Richards bought the entire parcel with the house. That would be 262 acres. Cassie? You there?"

"Yes, I'm here." Cassie racked her brain, trying to remember the circumstances of the sale. She already knew that after Great-Grandfather McClure died, Lorraine moved in with Eva and Harlon. But she didn't know why. Was Lorraine incapable of taking care of herself out in the country alone? Did she have a nervous breakdown after her husband died?

Something told Cassie that Eva and Harlon had tricked Lorraine into selling. Or maybe they convinced Lorraine it was for her own good to sell and move into the Tudor House.

"Thank you, Brian," she said. "Do you happen to know how old the Richards are and if they have children?"

Cassie could hear him flipping through his notes. "They're elderly," he said. "Brenden, the husband, is five years older than his wife. He's ninety-two."

"Do they have kids?"

"No kids. I did find out by asking around that Brenden was admitted to the Guernsey County Hospital two days ago. He had a stroke when he was outside in the barn and fell and broke a hip."

Everyone knew that when an elderly person broke a hip, other limbs and sometimes organs closed down next. At the very least, it was difficult to mend fragile bones.

"I'll keep an eye on things," said Brian. "How about dinner tonight?"

She was taken off guard by the dinner proposal. "Dinner? I'm really busy," she said.

"I'd like to show you some figures I came up with on your house. I have some ideas for viewings too that I think you'll like."

"I don't know—"

"I'll pick you up at your grandmother's on Everly in about—"

"No, I'll meet you at my house. In 45 minutes." Cassie pressed the end-call button without waiting for his reply. She started to panic. There was no denying that she was attracted to Brian, maybe even more than she was attracted to Eric.

But she kept thinking about Eric; even when she woke up in the morning, her first thoughts were of Eric.

She would change clothes and meet Brian O'Dea—for business purposes only.

But after she went back upstairs to her bedroom to get her handbag and change her blouse and jeans, she heard voices. One was definitely Frances's and she could swear, if memory served her right, that the other was Grandfather Harlon's.

CHAPTER 24

Harlon was furious that Eva would not add his name to the deed of the Tudor House. After all, as he mentioned often, "The house was a wedding gift to *us*, not just you!"

"I'm sorry, Harlon," Eva would say on her way out of the house to run errands or to the kitchen to begin dinner preparations. "I think it's best to leave things the way they are."

"I don't! I want my name added. It's *our* home!" At this point in the conversation Harlon would normally retreat, but it was imperative to talk Eva into adding his name to the deed before he left for Columbus to meet Harold Larrabee. He could mortgage the property and have plenty of funds to invest with Harold on several of his up-and-coming building ventures. Or at the very least, as a property owner, he would secure leverage.

Yet Eva wouldn't budge.

Harlon wondered if he could forge her signature. That might be the only way around her controlling behavior. Why was she so stubborn, especially after almost thirty years of marriage? Why would the old man, Ian McClure, who Harlon admired and thought of as a father figure, a mentor in business, give the extraordinary gift to Eva only?

Harlon called Roy to tell him he was going on a four- or five-day business trip to Cleveland. He would contact him when he returned. *Look after your mother while I'm away,* he said.

He packed enough clothes for a week. One never knew how long the business trips would take, especially "business rendezvous" with Harold Larrabee, and because Eva had forced his hand by refusing to add his name to the deed, he would go to a jeweler in Columbus while visiting Harold. Over the past few weeks, Harlon had broken into Eva's favorite jewelry box. He stole an emerald and diamond necklace that was once Lorraine's. A pity he couldn't find the ring that matched the necklace. In Eva's dresser, in the middle drawer in the back behind her lingerie and miscellaneous silk scarves and handkerchiefs, he found a velvet box containing a collection of rings. He stole two diamond rings and two sapphire rings Lorraine had given her. He also stole three strands of authentic pearls.

He knew the *really* good stuff was locked away in a safe-deposit box at the bank.

This cache of treasures would bring a substantial amount of cash—as long as he found the right jeweler in Columbus. If he had to, he would go to Cleveland on his search, or even New York City. There was no limit to Harlon's quest to impress Harold Larrabee.

Harold Larrabee was waiting for Harlon at the bus station. Harlon was adamant about not taking his personal car on business trips. He always said that if he used public transportation, no one would be able to identify a vehicle. There would be no license plate to trace, no gas receipts to acquire in order to tally up his credit cards. It was safer and smarter, he said, to travel by bus or plane.

When Harlon stepped off the bus, he was light-headed and even lighter of step, thanks to the three bourbon and colas he drank during the ride from Cambridge to Columbus. Harold, as if sensing Harlon was intoxicated, smiled seductively, showing two gold-capped teeth and a nickel-sized dimple at the side of his mouth.

Harold was dressed sharply, as always. He wore the best clothing money could buy, from his stylish silk beret to his custom-made Italian shoes. His cashmere suit was tailored specifically for him, as were all of his suits, but because of the heat, he didn't wear the jacket, just the pinstriped vest, white shirt, and trousers.

He came toward Harlon with an outstretched arm, but Harlon was a *married* man and guarded his privacy.

"Harlon!" He beamed, his breath blazing of liquor. "I can't believe you're finally here! It's so good to see you!"

Harlon wanted to mention that they recently had lunch together at Buckeye Lake and discussed buying a cottage, but why bother? Harold would always be high-strung and loud. He would always demand attention from every angle.

"Did you leave our dear Eva to her own devices?" Harold said with a wink.

Harlon tried to knock Harold's arm off his shoulder with his elbow. "Yes. In fact, she's visiting friends. I have no idea where, and I could care less."

"Oh," Harold pouted, his lips bulging. "She still won't put your name on the deed?"

"No, the malicious cow won't even consider it."

"Her father probably told her not to, Harlon." Harold tried to grab Harlon's hand but Harlon stepped to the side. "I knew McClure and he was a man of principle. He was also a fiercely loyal and family-oriented man. I mean by blood. Irish blood, precisely. This loyalty has filtered down to his only child, I'm quite sure."

"You seem to know a lot about her!" Harlon yelled, walking at a fast clip.

"You *assume* so," Harold said, shrugging.

"I don't want to talk about it here!" Harlon carried his suitcase with one hand and gave Harold his briefcase with the other. He opened the taxi door and waited patiently for Harlon to climb inside the back seat.

Once inside the cab, Harold put his hand on Harlon's knee and turned his head for a kiss on the mouth. The taxi driver asked where to, and Harold told him—the Hyatt—whereby Harold kissed Harlon again, this time harder and with a probing tongue.

• • •

Once they were secluded in the hotel room, Harlon played along with the kissing and fondling. Harold poured them each a glass of champagne. He toasted their union, their ability to sneak in three meetings within the past month. Harold always met Harlon either at an airport or a bus station. They stayed in expensive hotels and ate outrageously decadent meals. They drank too much and stayed up too late. Kissed and drilled each other until they were both raw.

• • •

Harlon managed to sell all of Eva's jewelry in East Columbus for twelve thousand dollars, enough to give Harold ten thousand for a new French restaurant investment; the other two thousand Harlon kept as pocket change.

He knew where Eva hid other valuable jewelry. She had a cedar chest that she *thought* she kept well hidden. Inside this cedar chest (she once told him it was a hope chest given to her by her mother) she hid thousands of dollars. Every now and then he lifted five hundred or so. She also hid valuable books and old coins that were her father's, and her mother's diamond engagement ring worth at least twenty thousand dollars. He knew this because he took the ring to a jeweler for an estimate when Eva was away visiting relatives. The jeweler offered to buy the ring but Harlon couldn't bring himself to sell it. Instead, he returned the ring to the cedar chest, velvet box and all. He would sell the ring *only* if he had to. In other words, she'd better put his name on the deed the next time he asked or he would have to resort to drastic measures.

Harold and Harlon were naked in bed together when the phone rang on the bedside table. Harold, apparently exasperated when he had to remove his hand from between Harlon's legs to answer the call, blurted, "What is it?" He listened carefully. "Uh huh, I see."

He gave the phone to Harlon.

"Mr. Hall?" said a male voice.

"Yes," said Harlon.

"This is Jerome Jaffney from Sterling Jewelers. A woman was here after you left inquiring about the jewelry you sold us."

Harlon felt a trickle of sweat drip down his bare back. Or was it Harold's wet tongue? "Go on," he stammered.

"She says the jewelry was stolen. She had receipts and documentation. I think you need to come here immediately and straighten this out."

"Wait a minute. Say that again, please?" Harlon had hopped out of bed, naked as a jaybird, and looking like one too. "Who are you again, please?"

"Jerome Jaffney from Sterling Jewelers. Here in Columbus. If you don't return my money, I will be contacting the police. Thankfully, the woman said she just wanted her jewelry back and left. As far as I know, she isn't pressing charges."

Harlon looked at Harold, thinking, *Dear God, what if Harold won't return the ten grand?*

Harlon knew at that precise moment the game had changed. Harold Larrabee would not only be able to seduce him; he would own him.

"What was this woman's name?" Harlon asked, although he already knew.

"Her name was Eva McClure," said Jaffney. "I suggest you get here within the hour with my money or I'm making that call."

CHAPTER 25

Cassie was so shaken up; she drove over the speed limit to her house on Eighth Avenue. She remembered Grandfather Harlon's voice—not deep, not high. Somewhere in between.

She couldn't bring herself to go to Grandmother's bedroom, or even in that direction, to find out who Frances was talking to. It was definitely a man's voice, and they weren't arguing; it sounded more like a polite discussion.

She told Brian about the man talking to Frances as soon as she stepped out of her vehicle. "I can't imagine who it might be!"

"Maybe your grandmother has a boyfriend," Brian suggested. It was clear he didn't know what to tell her. "Or this Frances person has one."

Cassie unlocked the kitchen door. They walked through the closed-in porch area and Brian flipped on the lights. "I forgot to make a set of keys for you," she said. "I'll do that today."

He was already spreading official-looking papers across the kitchen table. "As I said, Brenden Richards is in the hospital. It doesn't look good. He has very little movement on the right side of his body and he can't talk. I have a feeling if something happens to him, Sandra, his wife, will want to sell. Are you still interested in the property?"

"Yes! In fact, let's go see it right now!" Cassie headed for the side door. "Right now, Brian!"

"Hold on a minute. Did you find those papers for me? The maintenance papers?"

Cassie paused to study him. Brian looked professional, and well-groomed even in the heat, but he was always revved up, she noticed. Always ready for the next step.

"I need the papers," he repeated, in a steadier tone.

Cassie was already standing outside on the porch. "I'll find them. And after we see the house; I'll make a set of keys for you. Let's go!"

• • •

This amazing house of my great-grandparents, thought Cassie as she imagined them standing on the front porch. As she pictured the parties, the dinners, the barbeques.

"I *feel* them here," she said. "My great-grandparents."

Cassie strolled through the yard, seeing her great-grandparents in their prime, with all of their friends. Ian was a debonair, charismatic businessman from Ireland and Lorraine was his beautiful lady.

Cassie somehow knew that even in her old age, Lorraine was well-endowed in every way, from her figure to her enchanting personality. Her long hair, brown or gray, was brushed upward into a loop and pinned to the back of her head. So glamorous and beautiful.

Great-Grandfather Ian: a stout man but endearing, enthusiastic. Genuinely happy to be alive. Any woman would want to be with him. Any woman.

Cassie shivered in spite of the heat. A current of sparkles drifted from one side of the tree line back to the other, making the leaves tremble. But there was no breeze whatsoever. *I feel you here. I know you're here.*

"My great-grandparents built this house," she told Brian. "My great-grandfather made a fortune in the coal mining industry. Long ago. He was from Ireland," she added. "He met my great-grandmother on his way here. They married when she was seventeen and he was eighteen."

"Sandra must be at the hospital," Brian said distractedly. "The car's gone."

"I wonder how long they lived here," Cassie said. "All this beautiful land. The green hills and valley. It's all so incredible." She wanted to climb the porch steps and look through the front windows. She wanted to sleep here tonight.

But she knew she couldn't. Not yet.

They had taken her car and left Brian's in the driveway on Eighth Avenue. She walked back to her car and climbed inside, knowing that it was time to step up the process of clearing out her house.

On the ride back to Cambridge, Brian asked, "Forgive me for being nosey, but is your grandmother happy in that huge house on Everly?"

"I wouldn't know. She seems to be. But there's so much space, so many rooms. Honestly, I get lost there myself."

Brian stroked his chin. "Maybe you should talk her into downsizing. Sell the mansion and find something more realistic. For her, I mean."

Cassie considered his question, his interest in Grand-mother's house and property. Now she knew for sure that this meeting between them was only business.

He wants a hefty commission.

It's part of his job.

• • •

After dinner, he invited her to follow him back to his apartment but she was too nervous to take him up on it. "I can't. I have to get back. Maybe I'll talk to my grandmother about selling her house."

That was all she was to Brian: a commission. On behalf of her grandmother.

He came closer to her but she lifted the handbag to her shoulder and walked to her car. "I promise to look for the papers tonight and bring them to your office by noon tomorrow."

She waved to him before getting into her car.

The entire ride back to Everly Road, she couldn't stop thinking about the keys she had taken from Grandmother's desk. She planned to sneak back into the new bedroom. By her calculations, Grandmother and Frances would be having supper soon; more than likely on the air-conditioned back porch.

She drove to Route 209 past the mall and toward Everly Road.

She drove up the winding driveway, through the array of vibrant red and white roses, rhododendrons and daisies, past the two identical rows of bushes, and turned on the curve toward the garage where she usually parked her car.

The sun was still brilliant in the sky, scorching the pavement and the tips of the grass, despite the delicate sprays from the sprinkler system. When she ran to the back-porch door, she could hear the purr of the air-conditioning.

She opened the door and was relieved to find Grand-mother and Frances sitting at the round white table.

Yes, having supper.

But sitting with them, sipping on a glass of wine, was Eric.

"I'm going to take a shower," she announced, looking straight at Eric. "I'll be back in a bit."

"All right, dear," Eva said. "We'll save you some chicken pasta. It's absolute perfection!"

Cassie wanted to run through the first section of the house and up the stairway, but the heat of the day had caught up with her and finding Eric on the porch with Grandmother and Frances had surprised her.

She paced herself up the stairway to her bedroom. First, she took the bundle of cash from the bottom of the box of clothes and stuffed it into her handbag. It had occurred to her that the sooner she deposited Grandmother Lorraine's money into her savings account the better. She would stop at the bank on her way to see Brian at his office. Next, she changed from her damp short-sleeved blouse and capris to pale blue shorts and a T-shirt. She combed her hair, that had turned frizzy from the humidity, and sprayed deodorant under her arms.

The three keys on the metal circle were in the front zipper section of her handbag. She took off her sandals and shoved them into her handbag. She slipped out of her bedroom, closing the door behind her.

She tiptoed down the hallway, past Grandmother's former bedroom, into her new one and over to the door near the desk. Of course, the first two keys she tried didn't fit, but the last one did. Her hands were shaking. She knew she had very little time.

She turned the key and opened the door. The first thing she found inside the door, laying on top of a dilapidated wooden dresser, was Grandmother's shotgun. *Interesting*, she thought, *how her shotgun disappears and reappears.*

Yet, for some reason, Eva wanted Cassie to believe that she couldn't find it.

There were six dressers inside this fifteen-by-eighteen-foot walk-in closet. Cassie opened the top drawer of the first dresser she came to; it was at least five foot tall and just as wide. There was nothing of importance. Only handkerchiefs and hosieries, still in their packages. Odds and ends in the next drawer, and the next one too. Strange things to keep, thought Cassie. Small metal boxes, all of them empty. A collection of multicolored pencils. Candle stubs, price tags.

She searched through four of the six antique dressers, two of them with drawers so warped, she had to pull hard to open them. *Junk,* she couldn't help but think. *My grandmother is a pack rat.* But the fifth dresser by a tiny window had writing tablets stacked in two of the drawers. Flipping through a tablet, she noticed writing on every page, like a journal. Grandmother Eva's handwriting. She recognized the slanted words in cursive.

Cassie took four of the tablets, stuffed them into her bag. There were also recipe books, some old and some were recent editions. Scraps of paper, notes, mostly in handwriting other than Eva's. To Cassie, it seemed as if the dresser had been filled up in a hurry with items crisscrossed and stacked.

There was a shelf behind the dresser. Piles of photo albums. One shelf with velvet boxes, large ones and smaller ones. She looked through the top one and found a string of pearls. Another box held a diamond necklace, another a necklace with exquisite sapphire and diamond stones and a matching bracelet. The smaller boxes, as she anticipated, held rings: diamonds, emeralds, rubies, and ten or twelve gold and silver bands. One box caught her attention. It was pink satin. She opened it to find a diamond ring exactly like the one grandmother gave her the night before her wedding to Lee. Cassie gasped. The diamonds and bands were identical. Eva had told Cassie that the ring was a family heirloom, given to her by Lorraine as it had been an anniversary gift from Ian. The three diamonds were quite old, Eva had said, and rare, and worth a lot of money. Eva told Cassie that Lorraine, Cassie's great-grandmother, would want her to have the ring when she married.

Cassie took the ring out of the box, tucked it inside her pocket, and put the box back exactly where she had found it.

Cassie knew Grandmother Eva collected precious gems and received them as gifts. But Cassie was shocked at all the boxes in front of her. There were at least thirty. Grandmother probably inherited most of the jewelry from Great-Grandmother Lorraine. Other relatives too.

Why would she stash them away in a secret room? Why not in a safe? Or a safe-deposit box in the bank? And why, for heaven's sake, did she have a ring exactly like the one she gave Cassie the night before her wedding? Are they both genuine or is one a fake?

Cassie put all of the boxes back in the order she had found them. She needed to uncover photos, documents, military and marriage records, not look around for more jewelry and money. There was a tall, green, iron box near a corner. It looked like a safe, but it wasn't. There was no lock. She opened the heavy door to an array of deep slots filled with photos. They were categorized: Eva's childhood, Roy's baby pictures, Roy's graduation, the building of Everly House, Lorraine and Ian McClure. Cassie's heart raced as she checked the dividers, sifted through the slots. She came to a slot in the back with five or six wads of fifty-dollar bills; behind the fifties were at least twelve wads of one-hundred-dollar bills. She found three ledgers and several pages with different handwritings.

And then she saw the slot entitled Eva's Christmas Eve Wedding. She grabbed the photos and shoved them into her bag. Thankfully, she thought to transfer her wallet and keys from her medium-sized bag into a larger one when she remembered to take Lorraine's cash to the bank.

Next came folders of documents—Harlon's military records, the same folder she had found down in the basement with Eric. She skimmed through this and found his discharge papers, four years after he had enlisted. She found his bachelor's of geology degree but put the manila envelope back. There was no need to keep and study his records. She only wanted to verify that he was in the army. His discharge papers said he was honorably discharged, so apparently, he did receive veteran benefits. She should ask Grandmother Eva about Harlon's benefits and if any of the benefits still applied to Grandmother after his death.

In a closet, Cassie found Grandmother Eva's clothing on one side and a man's on the other. It wasn't so unusual to keep your dead spouse's clothes, even his or her shoes, which Cassie noticed were lined up on the floor beneath the hanging clothes. And as her father Roy had said many times, his parents were almost the same height.

Cassie knew she was running out of time. She wanted to find pictures of her grandparents' wedding. Not only did she need to see what they looked like when they were young; she also wanted a glimpse of the McClure Homestead on the day of their marriage.

She went to the unique iron box and searched the slots again, hoping to find more pictures of the McClure Homestead. Again, she skimmed through the large envelopes, several of them stained. The envelopes encased old photos and documents. She found an envelope with McClure written in blocky letters on the outside. She folded the envelope carefully and shoved it into her bag, now heavy with clues. She took two of the packets of one-hundred-dollar bills.

She wanted to take more of the jewelry on her way out of the walk-in closet but knew that would be pushing things.

She hurried out of the closet and locked the door behind her. She put the keys back into the middle desk drawer. If she needed to break into the hidden room again, she knew where to find the keys.

And something pushed her to hurry, to get out of Grandmother Eva's bedroom quickly, taking her bag of treasures with her.

Finally, she had pictures of the McClure Homestead.

One day, she would buy it.

She would buy it back for Lorraine McClure.

CHAPTER 26

"I don't know what to do, Harold! Tell me! Tell me what I should do! Eva was at the jewelers! She got all of the jewelry back! Now the jeweler wants his money returned! What the hell will I do?"

Harold simply stared at him. He was still naked, partially covered with a sheet. He was stunned, or at least his sagging face said as much. "I don't know, Harlon. I just don't know."

Harlon paced while attempting to put his underwear back on. He almost tripped. He reached for a sock, not even registering what he was doing.

"I need the money back. You must write a check to me for the ten thousand I gave you last night!"

Harold stood up, completely naked. He grabbed the sheet again and attempted to wrap it around his middle. "Sorry. I can't do that."

"What do you mean?" Harlon took a step forward. "Look at me! The jeweler wants the money back. Today. Eva was there right after I left with proof of purchase. Proof of ownership! I don't have that kind of money at hand. I gave you ten thousand to invest, remember? Just last evening. I need it back!"

"I already invested it, dear." Harold somehow latched the sheet around his person and lit a cigarette. Little gray clouds of smoke lifted into the air. "But I wouldn't give it back, even if I could."

Harlon was awestruck by Harold's remark. Harlon stood frozen, clad in briefs and one sock. He shook his head. He started to swing his arms back and forth, watching Harold Larrabee sit on the edge of the king-sized bed, smoking the thin cigarette.

Larrabee watched the smoke rise and fan out toward the corners of the suite.

"I need the money!" Harlon said in a squeezed voice, not pleading but insisting. "I had no idea Eva knew I had taken the jewelry. No idea she followed me here."

"That's a shame." Harold looked up at Harlon with an "oh well" expression across his creaseless face. "You took the lady for granted. I tried to tell you the daughter of Ian McClure is savvy. Didn't I?"

"Frances was supposed to cover my back!" Harlon shouted. "She works for me. She said she would make sure Eva was out of the house!"

"I wouldn't trust that ugly bitch as far as I could throw her. How many times do I have to warn you about stupid women like Frances Winthrop?"

"*Warn* me? She works for us at the Everly House. You know that. She's our maid and she's Eva's assistant. I shouldn't have to explain the help to you of all people!"

Harold snickered. He took another puff. He held the cigarette out and studied it. "You fuck her, Harlon. I'm not dense."

"I what?" Harlon shouted. "You're out of your mind! You've had too much to drink! And you're imagining things.

You're the only one for me. How many times do I have to tell you that?"

"Sure, I'm the only one." With that, Harold stood up. He dropped the cigarette into a glass of water. He dropped the sheet as well. "Service me," he demanded. "Do me and I'll help you out. This once."

• • •

Harold wanted it rough. Never before in their relationship had he forced brutal pressure on Harlon. He made Harlon touch him everywhere . . . slowly, deliberately. He made Harlon lick him up and down his entire bare body and back again. He shoved Harlon's face between his legs and kept him there, slobbering and sucking.

Harlon couldn't breathe. He was losing strength in his arms. His neck was cramping and so were his hands. He had never been handled in this manner— for so long. He thought he was going to pass out.

"I can't breathe," he said. "I'm going to be sick."

"Keep going," said Harold.

Harold grabbed Harlon's hair and steered him back to his crotch, made him stay there. Harold feasted deeply of the pleasure. He closed his eyes and whimpered.

"You and that ugly bitch," he moaned several times. "How could you betray me?"

"Please, Harold! I'm going to be sick! I can't breathe!"

"Keep going!" Harold yelled.

When they were done, Harlon thought he was having a heart attack. He started to cry. He couldn't help it; he was overwhelmed with humiliation and Harold's switch in personality, as if Harold had turned psychotic. Never before had he treated Harlon with anything other than respect.

Harlon watched Harold get dressed. Harold whistled as he pulled on his trousers, buttoned his shirt.

Harlon couldn't get out of bed. He felt completely violated and he was bleeding. He covered his eyes with his hands. He was so distraught, so upset that he had allowed Harold to abuse him, he wanted to die.

But he had to pay back the jeweler or he was finished. If he knew one thing about Eva McClure it was that she wouldn't let him get away with stealing family heirlooms. She was fiercely, soulfully, attached to her roots.

Harlon uncovered his eyes when he realized the room was silent except for the drone of fans spinning from the ceiling.

Harold was dressed and had combed gel through his hair until it pressed against his head, handsomely.

He is indeed a handsome man.

Harlon couldn't believe Harold had reached orgasm twice while enjoying Harlon's horrendous ordeal of panting and crying. Thinking of it made him sick.

"Harold," he cried.

His eyes closed when tears began to fall again. "Harold," he repeated in a broken whisper.

Harold adjusted the sparkling cufflinks at the wrists of his crisp white shirt. He said cheerfully, "Yes?"

"The money. I need it."

Harold moved for the door. He had a briefcase in one hand, a suitcase in the other. To Harlon, who had finally opened his eyes, it looked like Harold was preparing to leave the hotel. And Columbus.

And Harlon. Indefinitely.

"What do you say?" Harold demanded.

Harlon sat up in bed. *"Please,* Harold."

Before Harold opened the door and walked through it, he said, "Well, well. I don't know what to tell you. Ask your lover Frances for the money."

CHAPTER 27

C assie went straight to her bedroom to compare the diamond rings. They were exactly the same—the same design and weight, the same three diamond stones. She emptied a small ring box, put the new ring inside, and hid both boxes beneath the clothes in her bottom dresser drawer.

She knew she had to change her outfit quickly and get back downstairs before someone would come looking for her. Probably Eric.

She fixed her hair: brushed it out, restyled it into a twist, and secured it to the back of her head with a clip. She reapplied her makeup: face powder, mascara, and a dab of blush. She changed into a lavender tank top and bluejean shorts.

As soon as she exchanged pleasantries with Eric, ate something, and said her goodbyes to the three of them, she planned on going back upstairs to her bedroom to read the tablets she found, and also study the photos. First thing the following morning she would go to the bank and deposit the money she had found in both Lorraine's library and Grandmother's mysterious walk-in closet. Next, she would take the diamond rings to a jeweler in Zanesville; certainly not Cambridge as everyone there knew Eva.

Last of all, she would meet with Brian O'Dea and give him the maintenance records for her house, but she would meet him only after her other two errands. Of one thing she was certain: she was selling her house. She would hire a moving and cleaning crew, keep only the furniture she needed. As far as she was concerned, Brian could now open her house to show prospective buyers.

Adrenaline pushing her, she descended the long stairway, surprised to discover that the three of them were still out on the screened-in back porch, their dinner party in full swing.

"Well!" she said, fully animated to match their mood. "Isn't this the party porch!"

She meant it as a joke, but no one heard her. They were too busy chattering and laughing. Eric was playing waiter, refilling glasses with white wine.

Finally, he looked up at Cassie and smiled. "You took too long, beautiful, and now I'm half crocked. I came over to see if you needed help moving things out of your house."

Cassie smiled back at him. "That would be great. We can start tomorrow evening after you've closed the shop."

"We saved you some chicken pasta," said Eva. She jolted upward from her chair as if preparing to go get it. "It's in the refrigerator. Sit down and relax."

"No need, Grandmother. I'll get it."

Before turning to the kitchen, Cassie motioned for Eric to follow her.

Frances shouted, "Bring more wine!"

Once they were alone in the kitchen, Cassie said, "So, now you're entertaining old ladies?"

"I was waiting for you. What took you so long?"

"I had to sort my clothes and find papers," she explained.

She rummaged through the refrigerator, looking for the chicken pasta.

She kept glancing over her shoulder to be certain they were alone.

Eric was more sober than he pretended to be out on the porch. He massaged her shoulders and kissed the back of her neck.

She wanted to kiss Eric back, but the last thing she needed was for Grandmother and Frances to suspect her affections for him.

"I'm meeting with the realtor tomorrow morning. He's going to start showing the house, so yes, that would be great if you'd help me move things."

"Sure ... I'll help," he said into her hair.

"I don't want Grandmother and Frances to suspect we've been— "

"Lovers?" he asked hopefully.

After finding the container of chicken pasta salad, she carried the container to the counter and spooned pasta onto a plate. She lifted the spoon, indicating she was dishing it out if he wanted more.

"I've had enough," he said. "Enough of those two old biddies too," he added, referring to Eva and Frances.

Eric followed Cassie back to the porch, just as Frances turned on the radio.

"There they are!" Frances yelled. "Sit down, both of you!" Frances got up and pulled a chair out for Cassie.

She motioned for Eric to sit down too, but he put up a hand. "Sorry, ladies!" he yelled over the blaring piano and violin music. "I need to get going. I have an early day tomorrow at the shop!"

"You forgot to bring another bottle of wine, Cassandra." Frances said as she swooned and danced to the music. "I'll be back in a— *jiffy!*" She sang the word *jiffy* while waltzing off to the kitchen.

• • •

Later that evening Cassie read:

Harlon is doing his best to get more money out of the McClure estate. All he talks about is investing in Harold Larrabee's latest hotel or resort. The other day, Harlon asked me for $40,000.00. He said the next project of Larrabee's is a big winner. When I asked what the project is, Harlon threw a fit! He said all I had to do is trust him, trust his instincts. If he didn't get his way, he would name drop my father. He would say, 'Your father believes in me! Why can't you?'

Cassie already knew Harlon guilted Grandmother Eva into giving him large amounts of money to invest.

She skipped several pages of the first tablet. (She considered the tablets journals—easy to read and easier to hide.)

Harlon is taking some sort of narcotic. I'm almost sure of it. No doubt Harold Larrabee and/or his cronies are supplying Harlon with these drugs. Harlon sleeps in one of the guest rooms down the hall. This suits me fine. He comes home in the middle of the night or the wee hours of the morning. He goes away on his so-called business trips and returns without notice. He might call me while away on his trips, but that's rare. Meanwhile,

Roy helps me with maintenance and financial issues. Harlon is losing weight. I wonder about his liaisons with Larrabee.

On the last page of the first journal, Cassie read:

I've noticed a second piece of my jewelry is missing. Most of my jewelry belonged to my mother. I am beyond livid because my favorite pieces are either locked up in my safe or in one of my jewelry boxes. Also, cash is missing, approximately three or four thousand. Someone is going to a lot of trouble to steal from me. I keep the keys to my jewelry boxes and my small safe hidden. The person in question must have taken the keys without my knowledge, made copies, and returned them. It has to be Harlon.

Cassie flipped through the other tablets. She was looking for Great-Grandmother Lorraine's handwriting. Two of the tablets were of miscellaneous scribblings—notes and such, to-do lists. One of the entries caught her attention. Again, in Eva's handwriting: "Go see attorney about selling the McClure Homestead. Mother isn't competent enough to make financial decisions."

I knew it! thought Cassie. They needed or wanted money from the Homestead sale. They forced Great-Grandmother to move in with them on Everly Road.

Cassie switched her attention to the big envelope marked McClure Homestead. Inside the envelope she found faded drafts of architectural drawings. The first blueprint was a small building, obviously the structure where her great-grandparents lived right after McClure purchased the land. There was a drawing of an addition— "kitchen addition" was written in slanted handwriting. The next page was the first section, then the kitchen addition, and two more squares—one entitled dining room the other entitled library.

This envelope was thick. Cassie knew it not only had pictures inside but bank records as well. There was a bill of sale. There was a deed and papers signed and stamped from the recorder's office. There was a letter from James Wilson, Attorney at Law, presumably Grandmother Eva's attorney. Cassie read:

Dear Mrs. Hall,

Thank you for your cooperation in dealing with the Richards' attorney, Mr. Bradley Kincaid. The Richards made every effort to meet your original asking price, but were unable to find sufficient means. They are very grateful to you for proposing a plan to scale down the price.

As you know, the Richards plan to spend the rest of their lives on your beloved homestead.

Enclosed you will find the agreement signed by Brenden and Sandra Richards.

Yours sincerely,
James Wilson, Attorney at Law
Cambridge, Ohio

Enclosure:

For the reduction of price on said property and home of the McClure Family Estate belonging to one Evalyn Brigid McClure Hall, heir of the Ian McClure Mining Company, Sandra and Brenden Richards do hereby swear to inquire if living blood heirs (direct descendants) to the McClure Family Estate are willing or wanting to buy said Homestead with 262 acres on Clearly Road, Center Township, Guernsey County, Ohio; to remain intact exactly as when they purchased it from the Ian McClure Estate. If none of the blood heirs to Evalyn Brigid McClure Hall are capable or available to buy said property, then sellers (Richards) are free to sell to unknown parties.

Dated: March of 1968
Signed by Sandra and Brenden Richards
Cc: Bradley Kincaid, Attorney at Law
Zanesville, Ohio

Cassie's hands were shaking. The Richards are alive. According to Brian O'Dea, they are alive and still living in the McClure Homestead. Per this formal document, when or if the Richards decide to sell the Homestead, they had to reach out to heirs of Ian McClure first to see if any of them want to buy it before putting the property on the market.

She fanned her face with the letters and documents. She put them aside and moved on to the photographs. There was a photo of the front of the Homestead, looking basically the same as it did the other day when she was there with Brian. The house had been repainted, more flowers were planted in the yard, and several of the trees had been cut down.

The next photo was the Homestead at Christmas. The photo was faded, but there were six wreaths along the fascia board of the front porch, another larger wreath on the door. *Beautiful,* thought Cassie. She particularly liked the snow on the ground. Lots of snow. The next picture was of the wedding day. The inside of the house. Cassie held her breath. Too bad the photos were black-and-white; nonetheless, she was able to imagine the red, green, and silver decorations of Grandmother Eva's Christmas Eve Wedding. There was a photo of the dinner table with a beautiful lace tablecloth across the surface and boughs of evergreens placed among the candlesticks. There was a Christmas tree in a corner with wedding gifts piled beneath it.

Finally, she came to the people pictures—Grandmother Eva and her father, Ian McClure. Grandmother wasn't smiling. Her arm was around the stout and bearded Ian McClure. Her dress was exquisite. The bodice was adorned with satin ribbon and pearls. The sleeves were billowed, not overly, just enough to add a touch of elegance. The material of the sleeves at her wrists were pointed over her hands. She wore a tiara decorated with a band of tiny flowers that extended to her hair, which was upward in a swirling bouffant. She was stunning but she wasn't smiling.

The next photo was of Lorraine on one side of the Eva, Ian on the other, both parents sophisticated, worldly, smiling. Again, the bride isn't smiling. Next came the photo of the bride and groom. *Finally*, thought Cassie, *a wedding picture of my grandparents, Eva and Harlon Hall*. Again, the bride stared directly ahead at who knows what or whom. The photographer? Harlon, on the other hand, was grinning-wide. *He was plain looking,* thought Cassie. He was slight of figure; the same size as Eva. Although the wedding dress was floor length, Cassie could tell Eva had on flats, not heels. There was a second photograph, exactly the same—Harlon smiling and Eva frowning. Then another and another.

But the last photograph made Cassie pause. *Something is wrong with this picture.* She studied it closely, wishing she had a magnifying glass. Yes, now Cassie remembers a detail from her childhood about Grandmother Eva's smile.

Her smile's wrong. It's completely wrong.

After all the years Cassie spent with Eva and the photos she had studied, Cassie finally remembered.

Grandmother Eva has a crooked top-left front tooth.

CHAPTER 28

Harlon had trouble waking up after Harold left the hotel room. He wanted to sleep and forget everything, even the pain pulsating through is body. He felt sick to his stomach but pushed himself out of bed, noticing blood stains on the sheet where Harold had molested him.

He found his clothes draped over a red valor-cushioned chair. By the time he showered and got dressed, it was almost noon. Checkout time. No doubt Harold left him with the bill.

He looked in the mirror above the minibar. He noticed two small cuts on his face: one on his cleft chin, the other near his left ear. Oh well, there was no need to worry about barely visible wounds. All he cared about was functioning enough to go down to the lobby and pay the bill, then off to the jewelers and explain he needed time to collect the money. He would say he didn't realize the jewelry was stolen. No, that wouldn't work. He would say he misunderstood his wife's wishes. She told him he could sell the jewelry, and then changed her mind. No, that wouldn't work either. Fine, he stole the jewelry and got caught. He'd figure out a way to pay the jeweler back as soon as he could.

Instead of lying back down on the bed like he wanted to, he managed to find his briefcase and search the room to be sure he hadn't left any of his toiletries behind. There was a *tap* on the door.

Harold, *Thank God you came back.*

Harlon knew in his heart that Harold would help him. But then he remembered the two hours of battering, of Harold moaning, squeezing, biting. Of Harold coming to orgasmic bliss, not once, but twice.

I hate him. He's going to pay.

"Just a minute," he said, thinking it only proper to make Harold wait.

He made sure all the buttons were buttoned on his shirt. He slipped his gray-and-black striped tie around his shirt collar and tied it. He looked better than expected after a night of terror.

He opened the door to blue eyes similar to his own. To a face reaching the same height as his. "Eva," he said.

She stared at him with no expression whatsoever. She wore a cream-colored silk blouse and a dark brown skirt. She had on diamond earrings to match the diamond and emerald engagement ring Harlon had given her. She also wore a gold Claddagh pendant necklace Harlon gave her for her birthday two years ago. No makeup, as usual, just peach-colored blush and lipstick to match.

"What else did you take of mine, Harlon?" she asked him calmly.

"Come in," he said. "I was about to order up breakfast."

"You must be kidding." Her words were so steady, he started to worry.

He told her he was going down to the lobby to pay his bill and then to the restaurant for breakfast. He wouldn't be long, if she wanted to join him. She glanced past his shoulder to the room behind him. "Where's Harold Larrabee?" she asked. "I'd like a word with that louse."

"He left, Eva."

"He left? What big project is he working on now, Harlon? What multi-million-dollar scheme have you mixed yourself up with this time?"

Harlon shook his head and chuckled without bothering to look at her. "Like I said, I'm going down to pay the bill. And I need coffee and something to eat. Care to join me?"

Eva turned on a dime. She pushed past him, her purse swinging as it did when she was on a mission. It was part of her angst, a prop for her theatrics. "What a disgusting love nest," she said, glancing around the room. "I can only imagine what you two *do* in that bed."

"My God, Eva. Mind your own business!"

He couldn't believe she lowered her purse to the footstool, covered her mouth with a hand, and laughed. "Harlon!" she said through her fingers. She actually bent over, apparently finding his words, his wounds, his secret rendezvous humorous. Harlon stared at her, shaking his head.

"Harlon!" she said again. "I knew from the beginning you favored men. I knew you met Harold regularly for sexual trysts!"

"Good for you, Eva," he said dryly. "Now if you don't mind, I feel faint. I need something to eat. Join me downstairs for breakfast. Or leave."

Now her face was passive, her blue eyes piercing. "You have to pay back the jeweler, Harlon."

"I'm well aware of that, Eva. I'm going to talk with Jaffney right after breakfast."

"You bastard," she hissed. "How dare you steal my mother's jewelry! You know how much she meant to me! How much her jewelry means to me. I watched you! I knew what you were up to!"

"Splendid, Eva. You're a great detective. Now move aside, dammit. If I don't get something to eat, I'm going to faint."

"Oh, what a shame! Poor, prissy Harlon is going to faint!"

This goading from Eva? he thought. *It's not like her to care what I do in bed or with whom.* But the jewelry, yes. He knew she would be spiteful over the jewelry and he didn't blame her.

Tears filled his eyes. He couldn't help it. "I feel sick, Eva. I had a very bad night and I am going to pay the jeweler back. I promise. You have the jewelry so you have nothing to worry about. Believe me, I will move out of your beloved Tudor House."

"Oh, you will indeed, Harlon!" she said in a vile, scratchy voice. "You will have absolutely nothing. I will cut you off and you won't have a dime!"

"I have my work," he said, briefcase in hand, ready to exit the room. In fact, he moved past her towards the door but she grabbed him by the arm. He couldn't get over how strong she was—like a weightlifter, a man.

"Let go, Eva." He tried to pull away from her, but she was right up in his face. "You have your jewelry back and I just told you I will move out! You should be happy I don't want to stay with you! I don't want a damn thing from you!"

"Liar!" she shrieked. "I never trusted you! I know you've been stealing from me for years. I can account for every penny you took! And I know there is other jewelry you've taken and sold. I know everything about you, Harlon."

"Good for you, Eva," he said again. "I have no doubt you do. I'll have my lawyer contact you as soon as I get back to Cambridge."

He shoved past her, nearly toppling her over, and grabbed the door handle, making his exit at last.

But he knew she was right behind him as he descended the carpeted stairway, past several well-dressed patrons, going up as he went down. He was so exhausted, so weak, and still in pain from his ordeal with Harold, he didn't care what Eva was up to.

He paid the bill at the front desk with a credit card. He picked up his briefcase and moved towards the entrance of the restaurant.

He turned, but she was gone.

After he ate a substantial breakfast and drank three cups of coffee, he felt worse. His insides cramped and he developed an excruciating headache. *This is a nightmare*, he thought. *And it won't end.*

He wondered if Harold had poisoned him. If drops of a poisonous potion had been administered by Harold, maybe for weeks on end.

Anything is possible, thought Harlon.

The bus station. He was used to Harold transporting him to and from the bus station and the airport. Now he was on his own, and he wasn't sure how to get back to the bus station; in fact, he had no idea where it was even located.

He would hire a cab.

He went to the front desk and asked the manager to call a cab. He needed to get to the bus station immediately.

He admitted he was sick. "No, that's all right," he heard himself tell the desk clerk who stood next to the manager, saying, "Sir, you look like you might need a doctor. We would be happy to call an ambulance. Maybe you should sit down over here."

The desk clerk and hotel manager directed Harlon to a chair in the lobby. They deposited him into the chair, although he tried to fight them and get back up.

"I'm fine!" he insisted, now worried he had lost his briefcase. "Find my briefcase! I need it!" But he couldn't get up. He thought for sure he had been poisoned.

Eva appeared with his briefcase. She said, "It's fine. I'm his wife. I'll take him to the hospital. Thank you for your help."

Harlon focused on her face. She was talking to the hotel manager. She put his briefcase down beside him on the carpeted floor. "Here's your briefcase, Harlon," she said. "Oh, thank you," she told the manager, who handed her a damp cloth.

Eva put the cool cloth against Harlon's forehead. She held it steady for a few seconds, then ordered him to hold it himself. He felt better, but his vision was still hazy and wobbly.

"Harlon," she said. "Harlon!"

"Eva?"

"Yes, it's me. What the hell did you take?" Her mouth was contorted in snide accusation; it was not an expression of concern, by any means. "Harlon! What are you on?"

"I don't feel right," he mumbled. He wanted her to hold his hand but she moved away. She said something to the manager, something about how she would take care of things now.

"Harlon, listen to me," Eva said. Her voice was loud enough to cut through the hubbub of people coming and going, over the luggage carts squeaking, the phones ringing. "I'm going to get the car and bring it to the front door. Just sit here and hold that cloth to your head. Hear me?"

"Yes, Eva."

"Make sure he stays put," Eva told the desk crew. "I'll be right back. I'm going to take him to the hospital."

Harlon closed his eyes and imagined ocean waves. He saw a beach, warm and sunny. He saw glorious tall mountains. He heard seagulls, and he heard waves pounding the rocks, over and over again.

"Harlon!"

Eva again.

"Mr. Hall," someone said. A male voice. The cloth Harlon held was taken away and replaced with a cool, damp one. "My briefcase," Harlon said.

"Right here, Mr. Hall." The girl in the black suit worked at the hotel too. "Eva, take it," Harlon cried. "Don't lose it!"

"I have it, Harlon."

Eva was irritable. She told the manager and two other people to help her get Harlon out the front door to her car. "Are you sure, ma'am? We can get an ambulance here quicker. Maybe you'll need help taking him there. We would be happy to…"

On and on the conversation went, a rush of static. Harlon sat in Eva's rental car. He waited for her to finish chattering with the manager. "Yes, yes, thank you," she said. He watched her through the side mirror. *You're so sure of yourself. You're so self-righteous. So goddamned intelligent, and let's not forget wealthy.*

You think you're going to ruin me?
Well, think again, you filthy whore.

CHAPTER 29

Cassie knew something was wrong. She couldn't quite put her finger on it, but she knew it had to do with the photograph—the wedding photograph of Grandmother Eva smiling. On the left side of her mouth, one tooth, the canine, was turned ever so slightly and maybe it didn't mean anything. Grandmother was a young woman in the photo and now in her seventies. Maybe she had to get dentures.

Upstairs, Cassie took her checkbook, wallet, the identical diamond rings, and the large stack of cash out of her bag and crammed everything into her purse. She hid the photos and envelopes of documents under her mattress, but grabbed the maintenance records to give to Brian.

First, she would go to the bank, next the jewelers to get the rings compared, onward to get keys of her house made for Brian, and then she would drive to the realty office.

She glanced through the maintenance and repair papers that were mostly in Lee's handwriting. Somehow, she knew Lee would tell her to unload their house. He would say, "You need to think of the future. Without me. You need to buy the McClure Homestead."

This revelation motivated her. She knew, if the roles were reversed and she was dead, Lee would do the same. She would want him to move on with his life.

She rushed to the bank to deposit the money. Her savings account balance totaled thirteen thousand dollars thanks to Great-Grandmother Lorraine. She deposited another four thousand dollars into her checking account. With the five thousand her father gave her for "helping her mother at the fundraisers," also known as a peace offering for cashing in her stock (she shuddered imagining the monstrous total on *that* transaction), she had ample in her checking. At least she could breathe easily when it came to paying the bills.

Cassie was particularly anxious to take the rings to Cane Jewelers. She walked into the jewelry store, recalling visiting it with Rachel many times. Rachel loved looking at the jewelry—the sensational necklaces, bracelets, and rings.

"Cassandra Sullivan, am I right? Can I help you?" asked an elderly woman in a brown and maroon striped dress. She also had a tight orange hairdo, a bent back, and a string of glittering silver beads hanging from her neck.

"Hello, Mrs. Cane," said Cassie. At first, she didn't recognize the jeweler's wife, who had aged considerably since the last time Cassie saw her.

Cassie had been here five years ago with Lee, looking at engagement rings.

"What can I do for you, Cassandra?"

"I need to talk to Vernon Cane. I need to show him two diamond rings; they are identical."

"He's in the back," she said. "I'll see if he's available to talk to you."

Cassie waited. Although she could tell Mrs. Cane was interested in seeing the rings herself, there was no way she would let *anyone* other than Vernon inspect them.

Two more people had entered the store while Cassie was detained at the counter. Suddenly, Cassie started to shake and her mouth turned dry.

"You want to see me, Mrs. Sullivan?" asked Vernon Cane.

Cassie collected herself. Confident of a quick reversal from nervous to businesslike, she said, "Yes, I need these two rings evaluated."

Vernon tilted his head to the left. "Let's go over to this area, shall we?"

Cassie moved to the left counter where Vernon had a magnifying lamp set up for inspection. He also donned headgear with a small flashlight attached. "Let's see your rings," he said amicably.

Cassie opened the tiny lids. She slid the boxes across the counter. "Hmmm," he murmured. "These aren't ours."

"I know. The boxes have the names of other jewelry companies—Dublin, Ireland on one and Columbus, Ohio on the other."

"Magnificent," Vernon mumbled. He inspected one ring, put it down, and picked up the other.

Cassie knew which ring was which. She was careful to match each ring with its respective box. The one in the box stamped Dublin, Ireland was the one Grandmother Eva gave her the night before her wedding to Lee. The one marked Columbus, Ohio was an extra box of Cassie's that she had emptied and placed the ring she found in Grandmother's hidden walk-in closet.

"This one is made of cubic zirconia stones, worth possibly two thousand dollars, but only because of the gold bands. The bands are real."

Cassie thought she was going to pass out. He was talking about the ring Grandmother Eva gave her the night before her wedding to Lee.

"This one," said Vernon Cane, taking a deep breath and whistling low. "*This one* is the real thing. See the genuine sparkle? Compare the two and you can see the difference quite clearly. I have yet to see such a beauty," he added. "If you ever want to sell it, come to me first. It's worth at least fifty thousand, possibly more."

Cassie packed up her rings and put the boxes back inside her purse. "Thank you," she said.

And out the door she went. At a run.

• • •

Cassie didn't waste time in Brian O'Dea's office. She had intended to leave the folder of maintenance papers with the receptionist, but of course, Brian came into the lobby just as she was about to leave.

"Cassie!" he said, his usual buoyant self. "I've been waiting for you. Please come this way."

Meaning down the hallway to his office.

He waited for her to enter the small, stuffy room, followed her inside, and closed the door behind them.

"Brenden Richards died last night," he said conspiratorially, as if the news was a national secret. His dark eyes were waxy and wide. "We'll give it a week perhaps. But I can almost guarantee his widow will want to sell!"

She expected him to add, "Isn't this great news?" But to his credit, he didn't. He did, however, indicate a chair for her to take. "I'm in a hurry," she said. "Here are the papers you wanted. Please start showing the house as is."

Brian nearly jumped up and down like an eager child. "Wonderful!"

She didn't care for his reaction one bit; but then again, she knew he had the proper enthusiasm to get things done. If anyone could sell her house within a month, maybe two at the most, it would be Brian O'Dea.

"And here are the extra keys." She thrust a key ring into his palm. "I'm going to clear out the rest of my personal things, but show the house as soon as possible."

She wasn't about to sit down. There was no time for sitting or chatting with a salesman of any kind.

She turned to leave.

"Wait a minute," he said. "The yard needs tending to. I can recommend a lawn service, if you like."

She thought about asking Eric to mow and weed the Eighth Avenue yard but decided she had other plans for him.

"Just pick a service," she said as she slipped out the door. "And send me the bill."

As she sprinted through the reception area and out the front door, she heard Brian yell, "Karen! Turn the damn AC on! It's hot as hell in here!"

And it was hot as hell outside too. Cassie was sick of summer. Thank goodness the first of September was only a week away, but still, this heat wave could very well continue through October.

Her goal, she decided as she jogged toward her car parked near the courthouse, was to own the McClure Homestead by Christmas.

CHAPTER 30

"Eva," Harlon moaned, "please slow down."

Eva appeared to ignore him as she maneuvered the rental, a gray Mercedes Benz, through the streets of Columbus. He knew she was trying to get back to the freeway. She told him weeks ago she was having issues with her eyesight and her sunglasses, sadly, were packed away in the travel bag on the back seat.

But wedged between them on the front seat was her purse. Harlon glanced down at it three times. "I'm taking you directly to the hospital," she announced. She worked her mouth from side to side like a demented person with palsy.

"Listen, Eva," Harlon said coolly. "I'm done with Larrabee. He betrayed me in ways you could never imagine. I admit I sold your jewelry; well, you know *that*, and thank God you got it back. But Larrabee stole all the money Jaffney gave me! I had it hidden and he found it. You must believe me."

She glanced over at him with a crimp in her upper lip. "Why would I believe *you*? Even though I always knew you were after my father's money, I never, *ever* dreamed you would stoop so low as to steal my favorite jewelry! And precious heirlooms as well! How could you?"

"Larrabee," Harlon shouted. "He put a spell on me. I promise you, Eva! I'm completely over him!"

Eva snickered. The traffic didn't seem to distract her in the least. She looked demonic—mentally and physically electrified by rage.

"I saw you take the last round of items," she said, shifting her eyes off the road to glare at him.

She shook her head.

And started to cry.

"Watch the goddamned road, Eva!"

"You bastard," she said through gritted teeth. "How could you *take* from me like that? Take away a beautiful gift from my beloved mother? Oh, I hate you! I hate you now more than ever, Harlon!"

"I'll make it up to you!" he shouted.

"Make it up to me? I tried telling you I didn't want to get married! You kept badgering me. You made me feel like a dried-up old maid. I shouldn't have fallen for your bullshit about wanting to help my father with the mines!"

"I *did* want to help your father, Eva! I *truly* admired the man!"

Eva stayed behind the line of vehicles, turning when they did as they veered onto a ramp, heading south. But once she merged onto the highway again, she was crying so hard she put a hand to her mouth, as if trying to damn her own emotional outburst.

"You!" Her voice lifted to a scream. "Worst of all, *you* let my father down!"

"Eva!"

"My father! God bless him!" she shrieked.

Harlon grabbed the steering wheel when she raised both hands to her face. "Pull over, Eva!"

She dropped her right hand to take control of the steering wheel, but her grip was weak and the vehicle wobbled over the center line.

She couldn't stop crying. "I let you into my life and you tried to destroy my father's company. And his family! You ridiculed all that is holy and dear to me!"

"Pull over, Eva!" There was a short lull in the parade of semis and cars, and Harlon took the section of wheel above her hand and forced her to steer to the side of the road, where there was a long building. Beside the building was a dilapidated barn and further on, a row of cement blocks.

He told her to park near the barricade of blocks by some oak trees.

Once the vehicle shuddered to a stop, he urged her to get out for a reprieve of fresh air. He exited the vehicle first and walked over to the trees, their canopy swaying in the delicate summer breeze. He put both hands to his hips and walked back and forth. Back and forth.

Eva got out of the car. She had a handkerchief to her mouth, which she slid over her cheeks and across her lucid eyes.

She strolled over to the abandoned building and sat down on a rickety bench.

Harlon, still standing in the shade of the oak trees, turned to look at her. He shook his head and wiped his brow with his shirtsleeve.

Finally, he went to her. He took her hand and lifted her to her feet. "Let's take a walk. Walk off this anger, so we can come up with a plan."

"The plan is a divorce, Harlon," she whimpered, looking away from him and starting to cry all over again.

He pulled her gently into the shade of the oak trees. "These blessed trees, Eva. There's so much beauty in the world."

Eva scoffed, clearly mocking his words. What did he know about the beauty of the world?

"When I was a child," he said, "my mother gave me away, as you know. I guess I have a lot to learn about trust. I need more time. Do you understand?"

He looked down at her. He waited until she met him eye to eye. Her skin was furrowed into crow's feet around her eyes and her cheeks were blotched crimson from too much crying.

He had no idea of the emotional upheaval inside her.

"Do you understand, Eva? I'm asking you to give me another chance. Even though you weren't faithful to me and I wasn't faithful to you."

She lifted her bloodshot eyes to the clouds.

"I shouldn't have married you, Harlon. I knew better. I didn't trust you then, and I hate you completely now. It's over. I'll talk to my attorney as soon as we get back. You aren't getting a damn dime of my estate."

He put a finger against her lips. "Eva," he said.

"Ever!" she yelled.

When she turned, he grabbed her arm. He pulled her across the weeds until they were out of view and pushed her hard against the barricade of cement blocks. She blinked at him. He yanked her to her feet and smashed her skull into the blocks, and then again.

One more time.

• • •

While waiting for Frances Winthrop, Harlon took the diamond and emerald engagement ring off Eva's finger and the diamond stud earrings off her earlobes. He pulled the gold Claddagh pendant necklace from around her bloodstained neck.

Frances brought the shovels. Long into the night, they dug a grave behind the cement wall, taking their time: night hours translated into better hiding opportunities.

Harlon stripped Eva of her blouse and skirt, even her shoes, and left her in cotton underwear and silk bra. They picked her lifeless body up together on the count of four and tossed her, not delicately, into the deep hole.

But what took even longer was covering her with dirt. Packing the dirt down with their shovels. Stirring the top layer, so it didn't look suspicious; and even placing six or so stones and rocks on top of the slight mound.

It was eleven o'clock at night when they finished. Once inside the rental car, Harlon changed his shirt and tore off his tie—both stained with blood—and put them in his briefcase along with Eva's brown skirt. He stuffed the shoes and blouse in Eva's bag and gave it to Frances. "Get her wallet and anything else of value," he said. "Burn this handbag with the blouse and shoes. There's blood on the blouse."

It was imperative to unload the rental vehicle linking them to Eva before they returned it to the airport. Harlon knew Eva rented her vehicles from the airport outside of Cambridge, the one between Cambridge and Zanesville. Frances would turn it in; they would assume that Frances was Evalyn Hall. She would use Eva's driver's license and credit cards for proof.

Harlon found Eva's luggage in the trunk: two small suitcases and a makeup bag. Inside the makeup bag he found the jewelry, along with each items' proof of purchase that she had used to convince Jaffney the jewelry belonged to her.

Of course, there was cash inside her wallet: roughly six hundred dollars, two credit cards, her social security card, and her driver's license. Also, the paper necessary to hand in the car to the rental office when Frances returned the vehicle.

All very good. Although Harlon and Frances had planned this strategy ahead of time, Frances had to wait for Harlon's call, and Harlon found the perfect opportunity to call her while Eva fussed with the hotel manager.

Give it five hours, he told Frances.

Eva was so insistent on unloading Harlon at the hospital herself, she didn't realize he had slipped away to make the call. He told the three people watching him that he needed to use the bathroom.

"You have the keys to the house?" Frances asked as Harlon drove. Her job was to remind him of what needed to be done, step by step.

"Here." Harlon lifted the key ring he found inside Eva's purse.

"Checkbook?"

"Right here." Harlon held up Eva's checkbook.

Harlon would get out in a town named Hebron, and Frances would take over and drive to the airport and turn in the Mercedes. Knowing that the family had to be summoned to identify the remains, the original plan was to pretend that Harlon Hall had disappeared. He quit his job. He left his wife and family.

A missing person's case was easier to pull off than a death with no corpse.

But they decided to change tactics and say he died from a heart attack. Harlon would need to falsify medical records. He knew how to copy documents such as death certificates, in case members of the family would ask to see cause of death.

Harlon also knew no one would question Eva. All he had to do was make family and friends believe *he* was Eva.

Still, he would need to forge her signature on checks and accounts. He had her social security number and he had already planned on digging a grave and burying an urn filled with sand.

To spare the family.

It was absolutely vital to their plan for Harlon to act quickly at the home of Dr. William Marsh, a surgeon friend of Harlon's. Harlon had to get back to Cambridge and the Tudor House as soon as possible after Frances turned in the rental.

Harlon looked at Frances when he stopped the car beneath a dim yard light next to a building. He could tell she was nervous. "This will make you a wealthy woman, Frances," he said before he got out of the driver's side. "And I thank you more than you'll ever know."

Frances nodded, staring straight ahead.

"Don't forget to burn her blouse and shoes right away. And get rid of the jewelry. Don't try to sell it; it can be traced. I'd better be able to trust you, Frances. Just remember, we're in this together."

"I know that, Harlon," she said. "But if Larrabee—"

"He won't," Harlon snapped. "Trust me, he's on to fresh pickings as we speak."

Frances sighed. "Yes. He used you and you used him."

"That's right." Harlon leaned toward her. "Now give me a kiss."

She turned and kissed him on the lips.

"Don't mess this up, Frances," Harlon said before he disappeared into the night. "Remember, I love you. I always have and I always will."

CHAPTER 31

Cassie was so confused about the rings; she hardly knew where to turn. She decided to go back to the Everly house and up to her bedroom. Maybe a nap would help clear her mind.

Thankfully, Frances and Grandmother Eva weren't on the back porch; they weren't in the kitchen, either. Cassie heard their voices coming from the living room. She stepped into the doorway. Grandmother and Frances were talking to a short, skinny man whom she estimated to be in his early forties.

He saw Cassie before they did. "Oh, hello," he said. Both hands were on his hips and there was a gray swatch of hair upon his head, and he had gray bushy sideburns next to each pink ear. He wore dark-rimmed glasses.

"Cassandra!" said Grandmother, apparently pleased to see her. "We're making plans to renovate this room and possibly the dining room. What do you think?"

Cassie didn't know what to say. Eva wore a faded cloth around her brown and white hair, and her hair today appeared uncommonly abundant, as if she had added a hairpiece to what was already upon her skull.

She wore yellow capris and a striped yellow, blue, and red T-shirt with a sweater in a much lighter shade of red draped over her shoulders and tied at her chest. Strangely, her left leg looked hairy below the knee, compared to her right leg, which was smooth although sporadically riddled with spider veins. She looked elegant and frumpy at the same time, and Cassie wondered which image stood out the most. Eva's sandals, however, were a scuffed up, dirty-white plastic.

But her face, Cassie decided, was the most perplexing—there was not enough Eva.

Cassie moved closer. It was probably just the peach-orange lipstick, she thought. Too bright, and not only *on* her lips, but outlined around them. And that hairdo—a big, floppy, tangled mess fused together by the frayed cloth.

Eva stared at Cassie with an idiotic clown-smile across her face. "Well, Cassandra. What do you think?"

"What do I *think*?" Cassie repeated. She looked at her grandmother as if trying to see beyond her skin. Wanting to climb through her pale blue eyes.

Just like Grandfather Harlon's.

"I think it's a good idea to spend your money while you can," said Cassie.

With this remark, Cassie studied Frances and saluted with the hand not holding the bag, whereby Frances shook her head. "Your granddaughter's drunk, Eva," Frances suggested. "I *told* you not to depend on her."

Eva cleared her throat: "Cassandra, this is Chris Henderson, my contractor. We are at the talking stage right now, but I want your input. And you know why."

"I do?" Cassie asked, belligerence altering her tone.

"Yes," Eva said. "You do."

Henderson, his face as crimson as the two reclining chairs by the fireplace, barged in, "I'll just leave these samples with you ladies and give you a call in the morning." He put two folders down on the coffee table. "There's all kinds of ideas with any style you can imagine." He nodded at Eva. "M-m-Mrs. Hall," he added with a stutter. "That's all I've got for you for now, ma'am."

"Thank you, Chris," Eva said in her sugary voice reserved for chitchat. "We'll indeed make some decisions and let you know very soon."

Eva followed him out of the living room and through the kitchen.

Cassie turned to Frances and squinted, but Frances ignored her by straightening pillows on the couch.

Upstairs in her bedroom, Cassie made sure to lock the door before she pulled her loot out of the bottom drawer of the dresser and from under the mattress of her bed. She needed to keep all the papers in order; all the photos too, and, of course, the money. Most of the money she had already deposited in the bank but she kept a substantial amount in the bedside table. She counted roughly seven hundred dollars yesterday before hiding it.

First, she took the rings out of her shoulder bag. She held one in each hand before hiding them in a box of papers she kept under her bed. She was shocked by the knowledge that the three-diamond cluster ring Eva had given her as a gift, a precious heirloom from Lorraine McClure, Cassie's beloved great-grandmother, was fake. How could Eva do such a thing? How could she make a duplicate and pass the cubic zirconia stones on to Cassie, wanting Cassie to believe the ring was genuine?

Cassie might have received a fake ring, believing it was Lorraine's, but by God, she was going to end up with Lorraine's homestead. One way or the other.

She opened the McClure folder and found more letters pertaining to the sale. Basically, more of the same: copies of the deed, the agreement signed by the Richards, a page listing mineral findings on the property, and the two pages tucked near the back of the stack that caught Cassie's attention.

In Lorraine's handwriting, she read:

I miss Ian so much; I wish I could be with him. I wish I had died with him. We've been together so long. We met at a store, of all places. At my Aunt Beth and Uncle David's grocery store in Cadiz, Ohio. Ian came from Ireland. By himself, and he said often that he missed his family. Well, a sister, Brigid, much older than himself (our daughter's middle name), and his father, who he wasn't close to. His mother died when he was fourteen. He came alone on the ship to New York City; behold Lady Liberty. So many people didn't make it there, he said. Sickness took them. Hunger and pneumonia, mostly. He was eighteen years old. I was seventeen when we met at my aunt and uncle's grocery store. I didn't see him again until a month later; somehow, I knew to go to the store every day, in case he came back. My parents lived on the next street over from the store. Ian recognized me the second time he came into the store, but I got the feeling he was only being polite when he nodded to me. It was pouring rain outside yet I noticed he seemed happy as he searched the shelves. He was singing to himself. I don't recall the song. He walked over to where I was standing by the pastries and asked if I wanted a donut or a turnover. I thought that was so funny. I laughed. He laughed. He said he would rather take me to lunch.

I don't feel safe without Ian here. I keep thinking about how we met and the day we got married and how I left my parents' home to go with him. It was awful, all the run-down places we lived in, infested with rats and insects. We rented some really dirty shacks, I should say, along our journey as he worked on the railroad coming through the area, and also hauled supplies for building companies. His dream, he said, was to own land, maybe ten or fifteen acres would be fine, and he wanted to farm it. He wanted to build a two-room house. But it turns out that the land we chose in Guernsey County, near Cambridge, was rich with surface coal. We started a coal bank. Sold our coal to businesses in town and to people we knew for heat, for fuel. Ian was able to pay for our land this way, 100 acres, and a year later, thanks to the motherlode of coal, surface and barely underground, Ian started mining the coal. And soon, we ended up with our own coal company—McClure Coal Company. Also 262 acres of land. Ian built my dreamhouse, so beautiful, and based exactly on my wishes, on Cleary Road.

After my beloved died six months ago of a heart attack, my daughter Eva and her husband Harlon forced me to sell my home. Our dream. And the land with it. I will never forgive her. I don't trust Harlon Hall. I know he wishes I were dead like Ian, but it's my daughter, Evalyn, I will never forgive.

Cassie couldn't read anymore. There was another page, also in Lorraine's handwriting, but she had to stop for a bit; her eyes had glazed over with tears. Her heart was breaking for her great-grandparents, especially for Lorraine. How devastating to be forced to sell her land. Her home. Cassie grabbed a white shirt from a pile of clean clothes and wiped her eyes. Finally, she was able to read on:

> *I want to die. My beloved Ian left this world and has gone to the next. He is waiting for me. I know it. My daughter, Eva, has been brain washed by that horrid Harlon Hall (if that's even his real name). My daughter and I used to be close. I think about the way she was back then; she would never do anything against her father. It's all Harlon. I sit alone at my end of the Everly House (that her father graciously built for her after she married, just as he had promised). I sit and read. I hear them fighting, all the way down the hall. Or even downstairs. They argue about money. They argue about affairs. Harlon wants her inheritance. He wants to sell this house too. Move somewhere else. Get rid of me. He said I should be in a nursing home. Someone else's problem. I know Harlon and Eva stole my ring; the diamond ring Ian gave me for our tenth wedding anniversary. It has three oval-shaped diamonds on a band of gold. I always kept it either on my finger, or in a silver box if I needed to bathe or help in the kitchen. It's gone. If I say anything, Eva will tell me I lost it, that no one took it. She'll say I'm forgetful. I would never, ever lose a ring given to me by my dear husband. I hate them both. They took my house and kept the money for themselves. And they also took my beautiful ring.*

Cassie was devastated that Grandmother Eva could do such a thing to her own mother. Sickening. Unforgivable. Cassie wondered if there were more letters hidden by Lorraine in the library where Cassie found the money. Cassie started to cry again and fanned herself with the two pages. *Stay awake and solve this problem*, she told herself. Why would Grandmother Eva save this incriminating letter? Did she even know she had it among the ledgers and pictures? Was the letter hidden by Lorraine herself, hoping that one day the right person would find it and discover the truth?

As Cassie fanned herself, she noticed something scribbled on the back of the second page. She turned it over.

Dear Eva,

I know what you did. You married that vile man and gave him almost half of your inheritance to invest in that scoundrel Larrabee's schemes. I don't know what turned you, what made you so desperate to fear him. He's having an affair with that woman you hired, that Frances Winthrop who claims to be descended from Scottish royalty. Such a laugh. Nonetheless, you have known about the affair all along. And you had affairs as well. Is Harlon Hall really Roy's blood father? I wonder.

Cassie couldn't believe what she had just read. Harlon Hall might not be her grandfather? He wasn't her father's father? Cassie pulled Lorraine's letter from Jeremy out of a folder and compared the handwriting. It was definitely Lorraine McClure's. Surely, by living in the Everly House, Lorraine would see and hear a lot, and Cassie had no doubt that the journal pages were authentic.

She couldn't, however, figure out why Grandmother Eva, or the attorneys, didn't destroy the pages written by Lorraine, unless she believed the contents of the folders and manila envelopes and all the jewelry were so well hidden no one would ever find them.

That no one would feel the need to search for old pictures, documents, and letters.

Cassie was so dumbfounded she couldn't stand up. She wanted to march downstairs and confront Eva. She wanted to threaten her, force her to tell the truth. Why lie all these years?

Why give me a fake diamond ring the night before my wedding?

CHAPTER 32

Harlon was well aware that he was born with an oddly shaped nose. It curved in the middle, significantly to the right, and the curve had a bump that was noticeable. He also had thick jowls that drooped.

Harlon met William Marsh when they both studied at Ohio State University. William went on to medical school and years later, became a surgeon. They didn't cultivate a strong friendship, but met for drinks now and then whenever they were both in Columbus.

Harlon hired Marsh to perform cosmetic surgery on his face. He wanted his jowls reduced, perhaps lifted, and rhinoplasty to smooth out the bump in the middle of his nose. He explained to Marsh that as he aged, he became more and more self-conscious about his appearance.

He also slipped into the conversation that his family was concerned about his wife, Eva, who had gone to visit friends but hadn't returned.

Harlon paid Marsh with a check from Eva's account. She had signed the check before she left on her trip, Harlon said, and he jokingly told him the money was a gift from her—to fix his "inadequacies."

Prior to going to Marsh's home in Hebron, Harlon practiced Eva's handwriting; he wrote her name—Evalyn

Brigid Hall— over and over again. She signed all of her checks this way, including her middle name.

The surgery was grueling, especially since it took place in Marsh's basement and Marsh didn't have the proper anesthesia or updated instruments. The surgery had to be done when Marsh's wife was away, and as luck would have it, she was out of town with her sister.

The procedure needed to go quickly. Harlon knew it was imperative to return to the Everly House as soon as possible. He couldn't delay with a recovery period, as Marsh had suggested.

Harlon's nose was bandaged where the bump had been scaled down, part of the bone removed and the skin re-stitched. The jowls were lifted and tightened and secured with several stitches as well. The critical part was lifting the skin, but not too high or taut to bring about suspicion. The idea wasn't to stretch his face but to remove the sagging flesh.

Additionally, he had Marsh inject collagen around his eyes to create a crow's feet effect like Eva's. Marsh didn't ask any questions. The twenty thousand dollars Harlon gave him, thanks to Eva's funds, was more than enough to eliminate Marsh's judgments and keep his mouth shut. Besides, as Harlon knew, although William Marsh was a surgeon, he wasn't licensed to perform cosmetic surgery.

"I'm concerned about infection, Harlon," Marsh said for the third time as Harlon, a bandage across his bruised nose and stitches around his eyes, handed over the check and prepared to leave Marsh's house.

He gave Harlon a bottle of valium. "Take these for the pain. But not if you're driving."

"I'm not driving," Harlon said. "I called a cab. My wife will thank you!" he added, keeping a straight face, more or less because he had no choice.

Marsh slipped the check into his shirt pocket and nodded in reply. Harlon moved towards the back door of the house, wearing the ball cap he had packed in his briefcase. "My cab's here," he said. "Thank you for your help, Bill."

"Thank *you*," said Dr. Marsh. "I hope your wife is safe at home by the time you get back."

• • •

But Eva wasn't safe and she wasn't home. Harlon went to a secondhand store and bought clothes: skirts and blouses, shoes. Meanwhile, Frances had collected some outfits and accessories from Eva's three closets. She was told to find all of Eva's important papers and most of her leftover jewelry and put them in the cedar chest Lorraine had given Eva as a gift years ago. Then she was to take the chest and hide it somewhere.

Harlon met Frances near a small town north of Zanesville. He paid the cab driver, knowing the driver was used to customers with eccentricities. Having kept in contact throughout Harlon's minor surgery and shopping spree, Frances met him an hour after turning in the rental, a transaction that went smoothly by using Eva's identification.

Frances and Harlon knew one thing for certain: for the most part, people are distracted with their own lives. If their jobs move along without glitches and detours, they simply go through the process without questions.

Now that the rental was back at the airport where Eva had rented it, after taking a cab from there to the Everly House, it was crucial for Harlon and Frances to pull off the next step.

• • •

"Mother!" Roy yelled, clearly not sure if he should strangle or hug her. "Where have you been? Father's hurt. Or he's dead! He was in Columbus, not Cleveland! We don't know what happened and I've contacted the authorities in Columbus, but no one will tell me a thing!"

Eva's face was bruised around the eyes and bandaged across her nose. She walked into the den, carrying two suitcases, with Frances in tow carrying Eva's makeup bag.

"Dear God, Mother! What happened to you?"

"I had a small fender bender, Roy, which caused my delay in getting here. I went to Columbus immediately. The police stopped me enroute to tell me about your father." Eva collapsed into a high-back chair after dropping both suitcases at her feet.

She noticed Roy was staring at her a bit too suspiciously. Therefore, she poured on the voice-cracking and the trembling. "My face is a mass of cuts, but the doctor assures me I will heal adequately."

"Doctor?" Roy wailed, leaning against the couch for support.

"Yes, Roy. The ER. I had the fender bender due to my shock after the police stopped me to inform me about your father! Then I had to go to the coroner's office to identify his remains! I'm an absolute wreck! Please get me some whiskey or something."

Roy turned to Frances. "Get her a stiff drink please, Frances!"

"Certainly." Frances looked at Eva and frowned as if saying, "Here we go. I'm back to being Frances the maid."

Roy moved closer to his mother and shook his head. "What now, Mother? Without Father? I just can't believe this!"

"I know. We have to be strong, dear. That's all we can do. I've arranged for him to be cremated—"

"What?" Roy babbled. "You *what?*"

"You heard me, Roy!"

Frances reappeared with Eva's drink. Eva paused to take the glass and sucked down half the whiskey before continuing. "I had to! He was so horribly disfigured! He was in a wreck, Roy. He had a heart attack and wrecked the rental! As you know, he takes the bus or plane on his business excursions, but this time, while in Columbus, he rented a car and—" She finished the whiskey in one gulp and feigned hysteria. She put the glass on the table next to the chair, grabbed at her chest, and started to cry.

Roy reached for her hand. "It's okay, Mother. It will be okay. But I can't believe you're drinking whiskey! Jesus!"

"No, Roy! It's not okay! He was highly intoxicated and had a fatal heart attack. Thank God no one else was hurt! And that Harold Larrabee creature! He left the morning before your father. What a sordid mess! I tried contacting Larrabee but apparently he's disappeared off the face of the earth!"

"I think you should go upstairs and rest. You said Father's remains are to be cremated today?"

"Early this morning. Which means it's done by now. All over; and I'm truly sorry, Roy, but I felt it was for the best. We'll have the urn delivered here and bury his remains in our Northwood family plot."

She realized Roy was looking at her curiously with his right eyebrow angling up his forehead. He was dressed sharply in a tan sports jacket and black trousers. He had shaved and eased down on that absurd pompadour. Not quite as puffed up and not nearly as much hairspray illuminating the surface.

He was folding something with his fingers. She couldn't see what it was. A square of paper? A piece of foil or string?

"This is just *so* difficult to believe," Roy said at last, closing his eyes and shaking his head.

Eva started to cry again. "I'm completely devastated!"

She could pretend tears easily, thanks to the bandages covering most of her face. Not to mention the whiskey.

"Your hair's been cut," remarked Roy, out of the blue.

"Oh. Yes. It was bloody from my injuries so I told the ER nurse to trim it off."

"I certainly hope you took out adequate insurance on the rental," Roy blurted. "You're damned lucky no one else got hurt!"

"Bravo, son!" Eva shouted spitefully. "Chastise me! Plunge a knife into my chest while you're at it! Call Frances back in here immediately. I want her to take me to my bedroom!"

Roy summoned Frances, who was waiting in the wings. He helped Frances guide Eva all the way up the steep stairway and down the hallway to her bedroom. He offered to help unpack Eva's bags, but Frances assured him she had the task covered.

214

Once settled in her bed, still wearing a cloak-like wraparound dress and black leggings that she sensed Roy had trouble believing she even owned, she said, "I need you to inform our closest friends and relatives about your father. Tell them we'll have a wake soon."

"I'll contact Brundy Funeral Home for you too, Mother. Make arrangements."

"No need. I already did that. I informed them of his death and cremation, which is taking place in Columbus. I already have a death certificate signed by the coroner of Franklin County," she lied, thinking she must remember to create a fake one. "Now just shoo and take care of your assignments!" she said, pushing at her bandages and straightening her messy swatch of hair.

"Shoo!" Frances mimicked, shoving Roy out the door.

Frances closed the door behind him. She was about to say something, but Eva stopped her by putting a finger to her lips. Then she whispered, "Make sure he's gone."

Frances opened the door to peer outward. "He's gone."

"Did you get the other clothes?" Eva asked.

"Yes, and the stage makeup. I put it all in your dressing table."

"Good."

"You'll need to stuff your chest," Frances pointed out. "She was a C cup. And those leggings. Really?"

"Humph," said Eva. "I haven't had time to shave my legs. Be a love and go get my drugs and more whiskey."

CHAPTER 33

Cassie and Eric moved most of Cassie's furniture across town to a storage facility. She wasn't sure if she wanted to keep the items or sell them. For now, Eric suggested the storage unit. They also boxed up items from her kitchen: dishes, glassware, dish towels, and so on. The appliances, of course, would remain with the house.

"I visited my dad the other night," said Eric. "He remembers Eva telling him your grandfather died in a car wreck. *After* he had a heart attack. And I think he said it was during a business trip to Columbus. Does that sound familiar to you?"

"My grandmother told me he died in a restaurant. He fell over dead at the table." She didn't want to reveal the having-dinner-with-his-lover part. Cassie was wrapping coffee mugs in newspaper and putting them inside a box. She wasn't paying much attention to the conversation.

Eric taped up the box she had just filled and wrote "Kitchen" on the top with a black marker. "Dad said she told a lot of people he died in a car wreck. Don't you see what I'm getting at? Didn't you tell me your husband Lee had a heart attack and died in a car wreck . . . in Columbus?"

Cassie stopped wrapping coffee mugs and looked at him. "That's right," she said. "That *is* what happened to Lee."

"Don't you think it's strange they both died the same way, in the same city?"

Cassie didn't answer him. She was hell-bent on getting her belongings out of the house. Brian had a showing the next day. He had a showing two days after tomorrow as well. Foremost on Cassie's mind was selling her house so she could put in a bid on the McClure Homestead.

Consequently, she was way ahead of herself. Brian O'Dea was trying to find out if Sandra Richards wanted to sell the house and property now that her husband had passed away. It was a delicate matter; one couldn't just ask a bereaved person, "Are you selling your home? I have one of Ian McClure's heirs interesting in buying it as soon as possible."

Another thing Cassie was obsessing over: she couldn't let anyone know she found a letter Lorraine wrote about Harlon Hall and her father. She felt strongly that if Roy found out after all these years that Harlon might not be his real father, the truth might destroy him. Such knowledge was better left unsaid.

Cassie was thinking about burning the pages she had found of Lorraine's journal. Maybe Great-Grandmother Lorraine imagined Cassie's father's paternity or assumed it was true only because Grandmother Eva had had an affair.

"I think I'll talk to Sandra Richards myself," Cassie said. "I need to know what her plans are. Brian says they didn't have children. No close relatives to speak of. You'd think she'd want to sell the homestead now that her husband has died."

"He only died a couple of weeks ago, Cassie." Eric was ready to take a box of dishes out to his jeep with other odds and ends such as lamps and rugs. "Let's load this stuff up. Then go back to your gramma's. She wants me to help the contractor move furniture around in the dining room."

Cassie stood up. "And that's another thing I don't understand. Why is she going through all this trouble to remodel the dining room and den area? There's no need. Nothing's wrong with the way things are. I think she's losing her mind. I can't stand it!"

"All the more reason you need to move out," said Eric.

Cassie was headed for the kitchen door with her last box of dishes and mugs. "I can't just abandon her but I have questions she'd better answer!"

Cassie didn't tell Eric about the diamond ring switch or the page from Lorraine's journal claiming Harlon Hall might not be her real grandfather. She trusted Eric, but she wasn't ready for him to know her recent discoveries. After all, he worked for Grandmother Eva.

• • •

Eva and Frances were in the living room looking through samples of woodwork and flooring. They were huddled together on the couch, chattering like school girls selecting prom dresses and hairstyles. They were drinking wine again, although it was quite early in the afternoon.

"We're here," Cassie announced.

Eva jumped to her feet. "Oh, wonderful! Eric, I need you to help Chris. He's in the back with some building materials."

218

"Sure thing," Eric said, and off he went to assist the contractor, Chris Henderson.

Cassie stepped forward to make a show of noticing their wine glasses. "Grandmother, drinking again? Tsk, tsk. I'd like to know why you have this big desire to remodel part of the house. It seems kind of foolish to spend the money and waste the time."

Eva straightened the front of her bright floral blouse. She patted her curly, and recently cut hair, which flipped up at both sides of her head.

"I need a change, Cassandra. It's long overdue."

"Seems a waste of time and money," Cassie repeated.

Cassie realized Frances was studying her. Frances reached for her wine glass, took a sip, and swallowed. She held the crystal glass as if it were a torch.

Cassie wanted to tell Frances to mind her own business but she didn't. She simply refrained from looking at her and kept her focus on Grandmother Eva, who suddenly stood up, straight as a statue, her eyes locked on Cassie's.

"I need to talk with you in private, Grandmother," Cassie said.

"I'm busy. You can see we're trying to pick out flooring."

"I don't care," Cassie said curtly.

Never in her life had she spoken disrespectfully to her grandmother, but recently, something she couldn't define had changed between them. "We need to talk! *You* leave us alone," Cassie told Frances.

Frances looked at Eva, and when Eva nodded, Frances slammed her wineglass down on the table in front of her. She gave Cassie a snide look, warning her to watch her back, watch her mouth, watch all around and every which way, from now on.

Cassie waited for Frances to close the door behind her before speaking. "I want to know why the ring you gave me the night before my wedding, the ring you *told* me was Great-Grandmother Lorraine's, is fake. I had it checked out. The diamonds are *not* real. Why did you lie to me?"

Eva positioned herself back onto the couch. "I saw Roy steal it, Cassandra. He stole the real one and replaced it with a fake."

"Steal it? When?"

"A month or so after I gave it to you."

Cassie wanted to laugh, but decided to play along. "You saw him steal it and you didn't stop him? I find that hard to believe!"

"I had to take time to come up with the best course of action," Eva said convincingly. "I wanted to leave it alone until I found out where he hid it after taking it."

How could a person look the other in the eye and lie so easily? Cassie wondered. "I kept it in my jewelry box," Cassie said. "I found another ring exactly like it and took both rings to Vernon Cane. He told me the one I found is real; the one you gave me is fake."

Eva looked up at the ceiling, obviously conjuring up what to say next. As usual, she was quick on her feet. "When the time was right, I was going to change them back. I didn't want to invade your privacy. So, I simply haven't done it yet. I was going to tell you about the switch, but that would mean telling you about your father as well. The truth about him. Not only did he cash in your stock, he stole your ring. I didn't think it would serve a purpose to tell you that your father is a criminal."

Cassie almost said, *Oh, but I heard Harlon Hall might not be my real grandfather.*

She kept that card close to her chest.

"Does Mother know this about Father?" Cassie asked in a brash tone.

"I doubt it."

Cassie moved closer to Eva and watched her mouth move as she spoke, paying particular attention to Eva's teeth.

"Do me a favor, Grandmother. Postpone this renovation project for a couple of weeks. My house is on the market and when it sells, I'm going to look for my own place. So please, wait until I leave to pursue these unnecessary changes."

Eva looked concerned. "Well, I suppose."

"I'm getting my own place and I've been job hunting. In fact, Eric said I could help him at the shop by answering calls and doing inventory. Temporarily, until I find a full-time job."

"Did he now?" Eva asked, crossing her legs. Suddenly, Eva's foot looked quite large to Cassie.

"Yes, he did. We get along *very* well."

"That's good to hear, Cassandra. He comes from an honest, hard-working family."

"I'm ready to be on my own," Cassie said. "Ready to move on with my life."

"Yes." Eva reached for the wineglass. "I believe you are!"

Cassie wanted to feel sorry for her but then she remembered there was too much mystery within the walls of this house.

"You need your own place," Eva reiterated. "I didn't expect you to stay here this long, frankly."

"Do you wear dentures, Grandmother?" Cassie asked.

Once again, Cassie knew Eva was about to land on her big fat feet. "Yes, I wear dentures. Why do you ask?"

"Because you used to have a crooked front tooth. A canine tooth to the left of your mouth. And the other day I noticed your teeth are straight. *And* larger than they were before."

Eva threw her head back and laughed. "I've had a partial bridge for several years now, dear. No more crooked tooth."

"You said dentures," Cassie said.

"I meant a bridge, Cassandra. A partial bridge."

Eva glanced toward the dining room area. There was a line of perspiration beaded near her hairline that, strangely, looked woven.

"What else did you find in my room, Cassandra? And how did you get the key to the walk-in closet?"

Cassie didn't like Eva's tone. "Frances," she said, standing up. "Frances gave me the keys and told me to take a look around. She said to check out all the treasures that will be mine one day."

Eva chuckled. "Frances? I doubt that very much!"

"Come on, Grandmother!" Cassie said, smiling. "Everyone, even Frances Winthrop, has a price."

CHAPTER 34

Eva grabbed Frances by the arm. "I told you to destroy everything. All of the documents, the photographs, and the diamond ring. Cassandra tells me you gave her the key to the walk-in closet in the new bedroom! She found the real diamond—the three-stone diamond ring! I hope to hell you burned the blouse and shoes like I told you to!"

Frances tried to pull away from Eva's grip. She wasn't as muscular as Eva, but she had plenty of strength in her upper arms. "I haven't had time," she insisted and stared at Eva as if she'd lost her mind. "Why would I give Cassie the keys? To incriminate myself? Do you think I want anyone to know what really happened? The little brat snooped around and found the keys on her own! I told you she was trouble! I told you not to let her move in!"

"You listen to me, dammit." Eva said, her voice back to its original pitch. "She was in *that* room, in the cedar chest! She probably found the other jewelry and God knows what else! Did you look through the papers and letters like I told you to? Did you burn the blouse and shoes?"

"The blouse? The shoes . . ." Frances said, thinking hard. She put a bony hand to her mouth. "It was almost eight years ago, Evalyn. I think so. Yes, I'm sure I did!"

"Go upstairs and check the cedar chest and all the other hiding places, the dressers and the folders!"

"Fine!" Frances yelled, spit hitting Eva's face. "But I *know* I got rid of everything!"

"She found the ring, Frances! The ring with the three oval-shaped diamonds. The real one! She took it to Cane's and had it checked out, along with hers—you know, the one we switched? And because you didn't get rid of the real one like I told you to, she found it and knows hers is a fake!"

Frances had had enough badgering. "I told you not to honor Eva's wishes and give Cassandra the ring when she married! I would certainly watch how you speak to me, Ev-a-lyn," she said the name one syllable at a time. "I'll not take the brunt of this." She grabbed Eva's arm. "For *any* of it!"

Eva, not at all rattled by the threat, said, "Go make sure the blouse and shoes were burned and check to be sure all the documents and journals have been destroyed!"

Eva hurried back downstairs to ask Cassie and Eric if they wanted to stay for dinner. She was determined to watch Cassie closer now; she had to keep Cassie on the right track. But when she got back downstairs, Cassie and Eric were gone.

Eva looked at Chris Henderson. "Where are the kids?"

"The kids, ma'am?" Henderson was busy going through the blueprints for the living room expansion. Even Frances had said that expanding the living room was foolish, but Eva wouldn't listen.

"Yes, my granddaughter and her friend, Eric."

Henderson rubbed his beard. "Eric helped me move some supplies out of my truck to the backyard and then they took off."

"I see," said Eva.

She walked Henderson through the kitchen to the back door. "I'll be here around nine tomorrow morning," he said as he left.

Eva didn't answer him. She couldn't stop thinking about the silk blouse. She remembered it had bloodstains down the front and on the collar. She ran through the living room and up the stairway, thinking it would be prudent to search the new room with Frances. If it wasn't there, she'd feel confident Frances burned it.

She found Frances huddled over the cedar chest in the new walk-in closet. Frances turned, nearly banging her head into one of the dressers. "You startled me!"

"Have you found it?"

"No! I looked in the metal box where we hid the blouse and shoes. I know I burned them, but it was so long ago!"

"Well, for heaven's sakes! You'd better hope so!"

Frances started to tremble. "I remember I wanted to get rid of the clothes right away, like we talked about," she said again.

"At least I know for sure the skirt has been destroyed. I got rid of the skirt myself," said Eva. "I don't really care about the jewelry. But we should go through all of Lorraine's papers. I burned some journals and most of the bank books, but there might also be letters and notes."

Frances continued rifling through boxes and dresser drawers. "I told you not to let her move in!" she said, her arms moving wildly as she searched. "And you let her see the new bedroom? *That* was a foolish move!"

"Don't tell me what to do in my own house!"

"I think we're way past that E-va!" Frances shouted, belligerently.

"Keep looking!" Eva ordered. "She found the damn ring I told you to destroy. Who knows what else she found!"

• • •

Eva walked down the hallway to Cassie's bedroom. She knew that Henderson was correct about Cassie leaving with Eric. *The two of them together*, thought Eva. *Cassie and Eric.* This pairing implied that she couldn't trust either one of them. So much for her loyal maintenance man, and yet, like his father before him, he had keys to every door in the house.

She would fire Eric St. James.

She listened at Cassie's bedroom door before turning the door handle. She opened the door slowly, as if expecting to find Cassie standing inside.

Eva was enraged when she looked around the room. Most of Cassie's things were gone. No more boxes of clothes and other items from Cassie's house. The bed was still made, however, the pink and white comforter spread out evenly on top of the sheets. There were clothes, blouses, and pants hung across the back of a rocking chair. There were types of shoes lined up in front of the closet, towels and sheets folded and stacked near the dresser.

Eva walked further into the room, thinking to herself, *this is my house and I'll go into any room I please.* But her mission forced her to be cautious. She knew that if even one item was out of place when Cassie returned, she—Eva—would be blamed.

Or worse, Frances would be blamed.

Eva walked over to the maple dresser. It was definitely an antique. She thought it came from the McClure Homestead as part of the Homestead collection that Eva had the moving company store up in the attic. She glanced into the oval mirror on the surface of the dresser and her reflection startled her. Her pale blue eyes were barely visible due to the stress of late which had caused her eyelids to swell, so much so that the crow's feet, the collagen Marsh had injected to puff up the skin, was now overly enlarged. There were huge gray circles under her eyes, due to worry and lack of sleep.

Her hair was a fuzzy mess, like a horribly bad wig that had pivoted to one side. She reached up and shifted it upon her skull.

Enough of her own reflection, she thought. *I can't dwell on myself right now.*

She opened the top dresser drawer, not much left but underwear and odds and ends like hair bands and makeup.

Her hands were shaking at the idea of getting caught. *In my own house.* The pressure of searching for clues had worn her out. Clues of where Cassandra had hidden evidence against her own grandmother.

The second drawer screeched when Eva opened it. There were papers inside: Cassie's bank records, business receipts, photographs.

There was no jewelry. Cassie must have packed it all away and taken it to Eric's place. *Eric, who works for me, not her.*

Eva sighed, exhaustion taking over her body. She reached up and grabbed the awful hairpiece stuck beneath the wide cloth band; it was so damned hot and uncomfortable, she yanked the coarse wig and hair band off her head like a hat. She inspected the natural hair beneath. Gray sprigs and pink scabs here and there, from lack of air all these days of wearing the cumbersome, itchy wig. The thick stage makeup, spotted here and there on the surface of her face. She peered at her reflection again and inspected the foundation that she applied every morning. *What is beneath it all*, she wondered. *I can't even remember.*

The teeth. She forgot about the teeth. The crooked canine tooth. Not there, no, no, not there. Goddammit, this oversight could cause the entire scheme to unravel.

After all this time, eight years.

She realized her teeth were too straight, both top and bottom.

Eva stood up, but in the reflection of the mirror before she turned to leave the room, she saw them—Roy and Cassie in the doorway, watching her.

Waiting for her.

CHAPTER 35

Roy's hands flew up to the sides of his face. "What have you done to your hair, Mother? You look … grotesque!"

Eva turned around. "Oh, my God," she said and almost collapsed.

Cassie checked the length and width of Eva's body. She was dressed in the same outfit Cassie saw her in earlier, but now everything about her, including her purple-blotched face, looked off-kilter.

Her clothing, mismatched and selected in haste, made her look like a puppet, maneuvered by something inhuman.

Cassie stepped forward. "What are you looking for, Grandmother?"

"I peeked in here to see what you are up to, Cassandra," Eva said without missing a beat. "I had a feeling you'd already packed up to move and I wanted to see for myself. I am *very* disappointed you didn't at least tell me first."

"I got a call from Brian O'Dea," Cassie said. "There's someone interested in my house. The person put in a bid."

"I see," said Eva. "What are you gawking at?" she snapped at Roy. "So, my hair is falling out. It happens to people when they age. Get over it!"

When Eva charged toward them, Cassie and Roy stepped aside to let her pass.

"Mother!" Roy shouted after her. "We need to talk!"

"Talk?" Eva spat over her shoulder. "I don't have *time* for talk!"

As Roy followed Eva, Cassie went into her bedroom to see if anything was out of place. She knew Eva had been looking, not only for clues about Cassie relocating, but evidence that Cassie had been searching the Everly House for signs of foul play.

All of the documents, jewelry, clothes, and other treasures Cassie had found were stored in Eric's office at the appliance shop.

Cassie closed her bedroom door and ran to catch up with Roy and Eva. She could hear them yelling downstairs in the kitchen. By the time Cassie got to the kitchen, they were sitting at the table sipping iced tea and eating brownies.

"It's just that you're acting very peculiar!" Roy insisted. "I sense that something is wrong with you. Something has changed."

Eva rolled her eyes towards the ceiling. "You've always been dramatic, Roy, even as a child." The entire time she talked to him, she stared behind him at Cassie.

Catching Cassie's eyes.

Finally, unnerved by locking eyes with Eva, Cassie walked into the room and up to the table.

"I'm staying with Eric until I figure things out," she announced, looking directly at her father. "I'm going to work for him part-time and go back to school part-time to finish my bachelor's in business. I'll be back for the rest of my things."

"That's wonderful," Roy said.

"Sit down, Cassandra," Eva ordered. "Let's visit before you go."

"I have a lot to do today," said Cassie, matter of factly.

Eva broke off pieces of her brownie but didn't eat them. "Fine! Then I want your keys to this house!"

Cassie found the key in her bag and put it on the table next to Eva's glass of tea. "If you recall, you only gave me *one* key. The key to the back-porch door."

"Tell Eric I want his keys too!" Grandmother said, picking away at the brownie. "And tell him I want to talk to him as soon as possible."

Cassie thought, *Good, give him his walking papers.*

Meanwhile, Roy shrugged as he finished off his second brownie and drank half his tea. "You ladies are being *very* mysterious," he said.

Cassie was pleased her father wore pressed trousers and a short-sleeved blue-and-white checked shirt. His hair was styled in the usual pompadour, but not as high and wide. He smelled of pine-scented cologne and he seemed completely alert.

"Mother," he said suddenly. "I agree with Cassie about the renovations. I think the project is too elaborate and expensive. I'll make up a chart with approximate expenses of each area if you like."

Eva glared at him. "I've already made a payment to Chris."

"I'll talk to him," Roy offered. "And get some of the money back for you."

"You can't tell me what to do!"

"I'm not *trying* to tell you what to do, Mother. I'm advising you." Roy had had enough of the brownies and tea. He folded his hands together on the tabletop.

"Why did you tell Cassie I stole Grandmother Lorraine's diamond ring?" he asked her.

Eva shifted in her chair. "I don't know. Your father took it, Roy, and I knew about it. I never returned the real one. Does that satisfy you, Cassandra? You have both rings now!"

"Why did he take it?" Roy demanded to know. "Money woes, I suppose?"

"Of course!" screamed Eva. "Why else! Your father was a demon! Why can't you accept it? I didn't want you to know the truth. But there it is. The truth, thanks to your daughter."

"I noticed you've never replaced Grandfather's headstone," said Cassie, stirring the pot. "You told me you had a new one made because the other one was damaged and the death date was wrong."

Beads of sweat broke out on Eva's forehead. Her right sneaker-clad foot tapped the tiled floor.

Roy prodded, "Mother, I think Father's marker needs to be intact!"

Cassie knew Eva was about to explode.

Eva jumped up from the table with clenched fists, although miraculously, she checked herself in time. "I will call about the headstone tomorrow, darlings," she said in a sweet voice. "After I go to the grocery store. Frances has tomorrow off, so I'll drive to town in the morning and get some groceries."

Roy stood up as well. "I'll take you to the store in the morning, Mother."

"Very well," said Eva as she turned to leave the kitchen.

• • •

At ten o'clock the next morning, Cassie met Brian O'Dea at the Eighth Avenue house. She was excited that Brian had a prospective buyer. The buyers were a family: husband and wife with two children in grade school, and they were in a hurry to settle before school started.

"The movers did a great job," Cassie said. "So did the lawn service people."

Brian walked through the living room, inspecting the floors and the ceiling again. He was showing the house at noon the next day. Later in the week a single woman in her thirties booked a showing as well.

Cassie searched the rooms to make sure she hadn't left anything behind. When she finished, she stood at the front picture window next to Brian. "I've decided to talk to Sandra Richards," she said. "I want to show her the document I found stating that whoever bought the McClure Homestead has to contact the heirs and see if they are willing to buy the property before the owners can put it on the market."

"Yes, you told me about the document on the phone the other day," Brian said.

Cassie braced herself for an argument. "I'm sure it's legal. Both attorneys signed it."

"I know," Brian said. "You told me."

"What's wrong? You should be happy you'll be getting a nice commission for this house and I'll hire you to help me buy the Homestead."

"Are you living with Eric St. James?" Brian asked her, boldly.

"Temporarily. But as soon as I buy my great-grandparents' house back, I'm moving in there."

"I see. So, you're just using Eric?"

Cassie laughed out loud. *Such a ridiculous question*, she thought, and such a serious look on Brian's face.

She narrowed her eyes. "Are you jealous? Eric's like a brother to me. Or a cousin."

"I heard you're way too close to be related."

"How about *this*?" Cassie put a hand on Brian's arm. "You sell this house and help me buy the Homestead. Then we'll talk about *closeness*."

• • •

Cassie drove out to the McClure Homestead on Cleary Road to speak with Brenden Richards's widow. Although it had only been a couple weeks since Brenden passed away, Cassie couldn't sleep for thinking and dreaming about the house and property.

She pulled into the driveway. The Richards had taken good care of the house and the grounds.

The red barn was attached via a breezeway to the right side of the main structure. Based on the photos Cassie had found, the breezeway was a fairly new addition. The large porch, almost the entire length of the front, was the same, but recently painted white, as were the balusters that were carved swirls from top to bottom. There was a large panorama window in front and two smaller windows past it to the left. There were also five windows on the second floor.

Cassie sat in her car, memorizing every square inch.

Then, Sandra Richards appeared at the front door.

Sandra stepped out to the porch, her hands on her hips as she waited for Cassie to get out of her car and walk up the stone-lined path to the steps.

"Do you need something?" Sandra Richards asked. She looked annoyed and distracted. She was attractive in an uncomplicated way; that is, her clothes matched in shades of blue and brown. Her hair, completely white, was styled into a small braid pinned to the back of her head. Her face was creased, but Cassie could tell she was once a striking-looking woman.

"My Great-Grandfather Ian McClure built this house," Cassie said proudly. "I don't mean to intrude, but please accept my condolences. I heard your husband died recently."

"I see," Sandra Richards said, her lips pinched. "You're here because you want to buy the house back into the family estate. I've already talked to my attorney, who apparently talked to Eva McClure Hall's attorney. She's already put a down payment on the house and lot combined."

CHAPTER 36

Eva couldn't believe Roy's attitude after they went to the grocery store and he brought her back to Everly Road. Roy, who was always preoccupied with his own problems, acted as if Eva was a puzzle that he, and he alone, must solve.

"I don't like what I'm hearing, Mother," he told her, breathing rapidly. "Cassandra told me you and Frances are"—he leaned forward, making an explicit showing of probable illness when he slid his palms to his knees, bending over—"lovers!"

"Get a hold of yourself, Roy!" said Eva.

"Cassie saw you two kissing! I never knew. I never even *suspected!*"

"We're not lovers," Eva corrected.

She was relieved he didn't say anything about the switching of diamond rings; of photographs; Lorraine's letters, one in particular that Eva prayed Frances had burned; clothing with suspicious stains; empty graves.

"We're best of friends," she explained.

She motioned for him to sit at the table.

"I'm worried, Mother," he said, pausing for air. "We've lost so much of the estate, stocks and bonds mostly, through bad investments. I know my father had a lot to do with it. But frankly, I blame you for giving in to him so easily."

Roy was clutching the top of a chair, both hands red from his grip.

Eva stood at the other end of the kitchen table, looking at him and waiting for the other shoe to drop.

"I couldn't help it," she said. "He was so sure of the investments. I wanted him to be happy. He'd badger me until I would give in. Even threaten me. And Larrabee—"

"Dammit, Mother!" Roy yelled; his facial shade now matching his hands. "I'm sick and tired of hearing about this Larrabee fellow! You both should have known better! Tell me the mystery between my father and Larrabee. There must be a reason Father was so trusting of him. So enamored with him!"

Eva felt fluttery and weak. She pulled a chair out from the table and slid into it. "Harold Larrabee was a developer of malls and apartments, office buildings. He owned restaurants and several nightclubs as well. He's dead though, so don't worry about him coming out of the woodwork to haunt us."

"His name comes up too often, Mother. I want to know why."

"It's just that your father invested in his enterprises, Roy! That's all I can tell you. That's all I know. Larrabee died of lung cancer four years ago. He isn't a problem any more, and if you want to know the truth, we *did* make money from seventy percent of the investments."

Roy remained bent over the top of the chair with his hands braced around the wooden edge. As was his habit when vexed, he shook his head and pondered the floor.

He suddenly stood up straight and turned when the porch door slid shut and Cassie walked into the kitchen. "You're buying the McClure Homestead, Grandmother?" she asked.

Eva touched her throat. "Who told you that, Cassandra?"

"Sandra Richards. I was just there."

"My father built it," Eva said.

Roy looked over at her. "What have you done now, Mother?"

"I'm buying it back, if you must know. I regret selling it."

When Roy lifted the chair and rammed it back down to the floor, both Eva and Cassie shuddered. "I've been trying to tell you, Mother! You don't have the money you once did in assets and accounts! You can't buy the Homestead back! Do you think I sold Cassie's stock for the fun of it? I had to! I needed it to pay bills and buy *toys* for my self-absorbed wife!"

"Roy!" said Eva sternly, back on her feet. "Why don't you just have a heart attack and get it over with! I'm sick of your tirades!"

She waited as Roy pulled a handkerchief from his back pocket and wiped his damp face. She continued. "I've sold eight hundred acres of land—near Center Township—to a housing development company. Land is quite valuable. I am using some of it toward the Homestead and some to renovate this house. If you don't like it, Roy, I don't know what to tell you! If you've squandered your own money away after all these years of a lucrative profession and bad investments, that's just too damn bad!"

"Rephrase that, Mother!" he yelled.

"Cassandra is the sole heir of my estate," she said slowly and articulately. "I changed my will last month. Signed and sealed."

Roy was sweating profusely and his hands started to tremble. He looked at Cassie, and she back at him.

He absolutely could not speak, while Cassie stared wide-eyed at Eva.

Eva could tell Cassie had something to say, but after Eva's announcement to Roy, she apparently reconsidered.

• • •

Eva left them both standing in the kitchen. She had said her piece and needed to leave the room before she lost her temper entirely. *Where's Frances?* she wondered. *I need her now, more than ever.*

There are tracks that need covered, quickly.

She listened in the hallway. Cassie and Roy hadn't moved, not even an inch. Eva could hear Roy's labored breathing, then heard him moan. Finally, Cassie went to him and said, "Calm down, Father. Things aren't what they seem."

"What does *that* mean?"

"You'll find out soon enough. Sit down and I'll get you a glass of water."

With Cassie's words circling in Eva's mind, Eva sprang into action. Fear was the motivating force of the moment: she had to find Frances.

Eva rushed up the stairs, grabbing at the banister like a blind person. She had to know: *What is Cassie keeping from me?*

And when she went into the lavish rooms she had spent a small fortune to renovate, she saw that the walk-in closet—the door to which was to be locked at all times— was wide open.

She went inside and found Frances against a wall. "Eva!" Frances yelled. "Help me!"

She saw Eric standing to one side of Frances with Eva's double-barrel shotgun in his hands. He said, "Come on in, Grammy."

Eva couldn't move. "What's going on here?" she asked, more to Frances than Eric. Now she wished she had taken the keys from Eric, weeks ago, when she first suspected he knew more than he should.

Frances had never looked so bedraggled . . . so deflated, ugly, and hopeless. Her hair was a mass of white threads, blown every which way. Her eyes were bloodshot. Her blouse was buttoned entirely wrong, the first button attached to the third one down and so on.

"Frances," Eva said, whispering.

Eva's hand went to her lips when she couldn't stop shaking.

She turned to Eric. "What *is* this all about?"

"It's all about you, Grammy," Eric said, a whimsical lilt to his voice. "You and Franny here."

"Where's Cassandra?" Eva demanded. She moved back towards the door.

Eric lifted the shotgun. He didn't point it at her; he just lifted it to his waist. "Oh, no!" he said. "Step on back in here, Grammy. Cassie and I have a surprise for you."

CHAPTER 37

Cassie and Roy left the Tudor House, errands pending. Cassie went to see Brian O'Dea. She explained that she needed to know the minute an offer was made on her house on Eighth Avenue. She was going to buy the McClure Homestead. Next came the attorney, but not the same one who made up the contract between the Richards and Evalyn Brigid McClure Hall. The matter had been handed over to his predecessor.

Eva's original attorney, James Wilson, had retired and passed most of his clients down to Stacey Barringer, who was now a partner in the firm.

Herein lay the purpose of Grandmother Eva's contract. The seller could only sell to a McClure blood heir, and if none of said blood heirs could be located or in the financial position or have the desire to buy back the McClure Homestead, then the Richards could sell outside the McClure family.

Classic Great-Grandfather Ian McClure's strategy, passed down to Eva McClure Hall, and now passed down to Cassie.

Yet Cassie still wanted to find out why Eric appeared so often when she needed him and why had he become important to her?

Eric explained to Cassie that yes, he went out to Everly Road to fix the gate without Gramma's instruction because he, Eric, was told by his father, Steven St. James, to watch for suspicious activities. His father believed after Harlon Hall's mysterious death, Eva was not the same. "Literally," he told Eric, "she is *not* the same person."

Therefore, Eric's father talked Eric into looking for clues—red flags, so to speak, anything out of place. When Cassie moved into the Tudor mansion on Everly Road and enlisted Eric's help to find out why one of the basement windows was left open, he knew that once and for all he would get to the truth.

Cassie gave the attorney a copy of the document she found in the new walk-in closet—the contract between the Richards and her grandmother, Eva McClure Hall.

Stacey Barringer was smart and perky, but only in a professional sense. She was older than Cassie by twelve years, and her intelligence and enthusiasm was brilliantly served.

Her eyes shined as she read the document. "I love it," she said. She curled a lock of her wavy black hair with a finger as she read further. "I bet there's a copy on file." She checked her computer. "Although it's a paper document written up by James Wilson, there might be a copy filed electronically as well. If not, I know right where to look."

Cassie didn't need Stacey's exuberant personality to light her own fire. She was excited about the document and also looking forward to her visit with a forensic specialist that afternoon. She sat and waited patiently as Stacey called her assistant to locate Wilson's files on the McClure family estate.

"This contract, although written up and signed by both parties years ago, is valid as long as even one of Ian McClure's relatives is alive. Very clever. Not a relative of the Richards or anyone else who might buy it in the future, but *all* of McClure's blood descendants. It's very specific and one hundred percent legal."

"Incredible," said Cassie, biting her lip and thinking hard.

"The document is so specific in fact; DNA samples will be needed as proof. Are you interested in buying back your Great-Grandfather's estate?"

"Yes," said Cassie, rising to leave. "And I'll definitely be in touch."

• • •

Although Roy wasn't important to Cassie in the traditional father-daughter sense, she wanted him to be with her when she returned to the Tudor House.

She needed his support in case Grandmother Eva became unruly, and she needed him to know the truth.

She called Roy and asked him to meet her back at Grandmother's. He had been going over paper work for a client, he told her, and the last thing he wanted was to deal with his mother again so soon, but Cassie talked him into it. "I need you to see something, Father," she said. "If you want to, you can bring Mother."

But Roy explained that Rachel was out with friends, as usual.

Roy arrived at the Everly House before Cassie. He was waiting for her in the living room, studying the supplies piled in a corner—materials and tools for the impending renovation.

Cassie found him pacing near the bay window by the couch. He was shaking his head and muttering to himself.

"Father," said Cassie. "I want you to look at this old photograph. It's of your parents' wedding at the McClure Homestead."

Roy seemed stunned by the sound of his daughter's voice. He stopped pacing, turned, and stared at her. He had changed into gray trousers and a red shirt that wasn't tucked in at the belt but hanging over it. He had on loafers with no socks. His heavy hair was smashed down the sides of his head. He looked tired and stupid.

"What's that?" he asked as she moved toward him holding out the photograph.

She waited for him to pull his glasses out of his shirt pocket and place the frame to the bridge of his nose. "Hmm," he said, analyzing the photograph of his parents, who were incredibly young at the time. "Lovely. Very lovely," he mumbled.

"Do you notice Grandmother's smile?" Cassie asked.

"Her smile?" Roy peered over the top of his glasses and then through the lenses again. "Yes, I suppose she had a very nice smile. Why do you—"

"She has a crooked front tooth in this picture," Cassie said. "But for the last eight years or so, she doesn't. And she doesn't wear dentures. What do you make of it?"

"Who the hell knows," said Roy, gearing up to complain about his aching back; his need of a nap. "I have no idea what you're getting at."

"Her teeth, Father!" Cassie insisted. "Look again. She has a crooked tooth in the upper front. Very noticeable. I remember it when I was younger. The tooth!"

"I wonder if—"

At that point in the conversation, they heard a scream from above, more like a screech tumbling down the stairway. Roy pushed his glasses back to the top of his nose. "Dear God, what was that? Someone's being attacked!"

Cassie ran for the stairs with Roy right behind her. "Who's up there?" she shouted as she climbed the steps. She heard sobbing, deep groans, and movement, like footsteps stomping from one end of the second floor to the other.

She knew that the noise came from the walk-in closet off of Grandmother Eva's new bedroom.

She went straight to the bedroom and to the door of the walk-in closet, where she saw Grandmother Eva trying to back out, but she was trapped in the doorway.

Cassie could tell Eva's hands were over her mouth. Eva stood entranced, not moving an inch. Not even turning around when Cassie called out to her.

Roy reacted in his usual spontaneous manner of action and moved around Cassie to the door. He took a hold of Eva's shoulder and pulled her near him until he could see for himself what the fracas in the closet was all about.

Eric stood calmly with a shotgun, not pointing it at Grandmother or Frances, but holding it to his side.

Eric said to Cassie, "They were looking for the silk blouse and black shoes, no doubt. We've been here all afternoon but they won't fess up."

At the mention of the blouse and shoes, Eva coughed up phlegm and braced herself against Roy as if she were about to faint. Frances, looking like a rabid bat, was pressed against the wall for leverage.

"*What* did you say?" Eva asked Eric.

"Cassie has the blouse and shoes," Eric said. "I told you, we found them weeks ago down in the secret basement. In a metal box. We had the DNA analyzed by a forensic specialist."

"Help me," Eva said to Roy. "Please, help me sit down."

Roy helped Eva over to a sturdy box and lowered her upon it. "You couldn't even do the one thing I asked of you," Eva hissed at Frances. "Burn that damn blouse and those damn shoes."

Roy stayed with Eva; his hand hot in hers. He nodded at the photograph Cassie held outward. "The woman in the photo, Mother. She's different. She's not you."

Eva laughed. "It *was* taken years ago when I was much younger!"

"She has a crooked front tooth. You don't."

Eva grabbed the band on her head and pulled off the scratchy wig. She wiped the makeup concealer from her eyes and cheeks with her shirttail. "The blouse and shoes?" she said, looking at Cassie.

"My Grandmother Eva's," Cassie said. "Like Eric mentioned, we had them tested by a DNA specialist."

Roy stepped away from Eva when she said, "I'm in the process of buying the McClure Homestead. Maybe we can work out a deal."

"No," said Cassie. "My attorney has a letter Grandmother Eva wrote when the Homestead was sold to the Richards. It can't be sold to anyone other than a blood heir. You're *definitely* not a blood heir. Not even close. We have proof. We had the blood tested on the blouse and shoes Grandmother was wearing the day you murdered her."

"What *is* this!" Roy yelled. "*Murdered* her?"

Frances, still looking dead and void, slid down the wall to the dusty floor.

"This is Harlon Hall," said Cassie. "He killed Grandmother and pretended to be her all this time. Eight years and we all took her, or rather him, at his word."

"Dear God!" Roy moaned, letting go of Eva's hand.

Eva? He had to bend down and look into her face. He studied her scalp: gray bristles, not even close to the texture of the hair he remembered on his own mother's head.

He kept staring, trancelike, but Eva, or rather Harlon, wouldn't look him in the eye. Harlon simply stared at Frances, wishing he had killed her long ago.

Cassie knew something about Eva had changed, but she believed Eva missed her husband and parents so much that her grief had morphed her appearance.

People see what they want to see.

Cassie dropped the photograph and touched Roy's arm.

She looked closely at Harlon Hall's face. "I want to know where you buried my grandmother or I'll take that shotgun and blow your head off myself."

• • •

Cassie didn't mention to Roy that Lorraine's letter claimed Harlon Hall might not be his real father. She knew if she showed Roy the letter, he would insist on drawing blood samples from Harlon and himself to prove it.

Roy called the sheriff and while they waited, Harlon wiped the layers of makeup from his face and neck. He took off the shirt he was wearing to reveal a stuffed bra and a hairy chest and armpits.

"The goddamned blouse and shoes!" Harlon shouted.

Cassie indicated the photograph. "I knew even before the blouse was tested. The wedding picture brought back my memories of Grandmother. She had a crooked front tooth. She was happy and smiled a lot, despite being married to you! The real Grandmother Eva loved her family, no matter what you did. Now you tell me, dammit. Where did you hide her body?"

Harlon sighed. "I have nothing more to say to you."

Cassie took the shotgun from Eric and shoved the end of the two barrels into the flesh of Harlon's throat. "Tell me."

No one moved; no one said a word.

Until Harlon Hall revealed precisely where to find Eva McClure Hall's remains.

• • •

How could anyone do such a thing? wondered Cassie after Harlon and Frances Winthrop were arrested for murder.

Harlon told Cassie and the state police where Eva's body was buried. Frances confessed that Harlon murdered Eva and that she, Frances, was accessory to the murder. The fact that the murder was premeditated would come out in the trial.

Harlon had lied to Cassie about the will. The real Eva hadn't changed the terms of her will, and Roy got the Tudor House on Everly Road and any properties left in her estate. Roy told Henderson he didn't need the renovations. He would sell the house, or at the very least half of the property, to pay Cassie back the money from the stock he sold.

Harlon's down payment to Sandra Richards was null and void due to the fact that he was not a blood heir of Ian McClure. No, he wasn't much of anything to the McClures except the cold-blooded murderer of Evalyn.

Roy and Cassie discovered that the grave they thought held the remains of Harlon all these years was empty. There had only been a marker and an urn filled with sand; this fact more than any other disturbed Cassie. She would never understand how anyone could pretend a loved one's body was interned in an empty grave. But back when Cassie saw that the headstone had been replaced with a rock, she knew something was wrong.

Cassie sold her Eighth Avenue house in November, thanks to Brian O'Dea.

She liked Brian, and Eric even more, but she focused on taking classes and finishing her bachelor's degree in business while working part-time at St. James Repair Shop.

Two days before Christmas, Cassie moved into the McClure Homestead on Clearly Road, and on Christmas Eve she decorated the dining room with strings of tiny white lights.

Outside, snow swirled on a gentle breeze as the pink and golden sunset spread across the hills. Cassie found most of the McClure Homestead furniture in the attic of the Everly House. Instead of setting the dining room table with linens and candles and ropes of evergreens and red bows as in the photograph of her grandparents' wedding day, she imagined it all.

So romantic, she thought. But also, very tragic that the young man standing next to her Grandmother Eva in the photograph ended up murdering her.

There had been two good reasons for Grandmother Eva to set up a document with her attorney stating that only blood heirs of Ian McClure could buy back the Homestead, if and when the Richards sold it: Ian and Lorraine McClure.

They were here in this house. As was Eva. The three of them stayed with Cassie every step of the way and would do the same if she ever had children.

Cassie sat in a chair near the dining room table, listening to Christmas music. She sipped on champagne to celebrate her independence. Celebrate her ability to buy back Lorraine's house. *They took it from you, Great-Grandmother,* she thought to herself. *But they couldn't keep it from you.*

Like the diamond ring on Cassie's finger, this land, this house, *this one* dream will always be yours.

Made in the USA
Monee, IL
20 March 2020